GIRL FOR HIRE

The Secret Encounters of Amateur Escorts
A Mischief Collection of Erotica

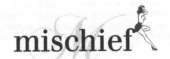

mischief

Mischief
An imprint of HarperCollins*Publishers*
77–85 Fulham Palace Road,
Hammersmith, London W6 8JB

www.mischiefbooks.com

A Paperback Original 2013

First published in Great Britain in ebook format by
HarperCollins*Publishers* 2012

Copyright
Best Offer © Rachel Kramer Bussel
Three Rules for Selling Sex © Lisette Ashton
A Red Carnation © Monica Belle
Sorry, Right Number © Rose de Fer
No Strings © Primula Bond
Don't I © Charlotte Stein
Substitute © Aishling Morgan
Appleton Avenue © Elizabeth Coldwell
How to Make Money as a Hooker Wife and Amateur Porn Star © Valerie Grey
Pleasuring the Enemy © Lara Lancey

The authors assert the moral right to
be idéntified as the authors of their work.

A catalogue record for this book is
available from the British Library

ISBN-13: 9780007534913

Set in Sabon by FMG using Atomik ePublisher from Easypress

Contents

CONTENTS

Best Offer
Rachel Kramer Bussel

'A hundred dollars? Really?' I almost choked on my drink as I raked my eyes over the early-thirties bearded guy who'd just offered me that measly sum to go home with him – and, presumably, fuck him. Not that I was actually considering it or anything, but still, $100? Even a make-out session with me was worth more. I wouldn't say I'm materialistic, but I like to know a man will invest in me, that he considers me worthy before I go home with him. Yes, I'll admit, I have a taste for fine dining and champagne, but I'm not a gold-digger. To me, it's a matter of respect more than anything else.

'That's all I've got,' the man stuttered, whipping out a crisp hundred and, from what I could tell of his wallet, the truth. A few stray dollars were all that were visible.

1

He didn't sound like he actually thought I'd leave the bar with him for a hundred, but why not try? To me it was the equivalent of leaving a waitress a twenty-cent tip; you might as well not bother, and if you did, you were holding out the cash more as an insult than an offer.

'A thousand,' a smooth, steady voice spoke from behind me. I turned to see a man who looked a good twenty, possibly thirty, years older than my twenty-seven, but he wore the years well. His salt-and-pepper hair was sleekly shorn, he wasn't balding and the slight wrinkles only made him look more powerful. It was his dark-brown eyes that made me go still. His eyes told me he wanted more than just to buy me for the evening.

'Look, guys, I don't do that. I'm not … you know.' For some reason, I couldn't bring myself to say it. Hooker, prostitute, call girl. I don't know why exactly, but even thinking those words made my face burn hot, and I reached for the water I was sipping in between drinks.

'Not a whore?' the hundred-dollar man asked coolly, an edge of impatience and something darker in his voice, as if he expected me to be one. Why? Because I was in a bar, flirting? Because I wore bright-red lipstick, the brightest I could find, to offset my pale face, and my low-cut lilac blouse did more than hint at my large breasts? Or maybe it was my snug buttery black leather skirt and knee-high black books that laced up the back?

Or maybe he just wanted me to be a whore, so that's what he saw. I nodded in answer to his question. I was mildly offended that he was only offering what I would make in an entire morning's work at my office job. But even more intrigued that another could so calmly offer up such a huge sum, what I'd earn in two weeks.

The bartender walked over and gave me an appraising look. I was, after all, sandwiched between two men who were close enough to me that it appeared I was intimately engaged with them, and one was holding out a hundred dollar bill right in front of me.

'We're all whores, darling,' said the older man, 'you just have to figure out your price.' I turned to make a smart remark when he pulled out a chequebook and handed it to me. Unlike mine, which simply featured the single stack of cheques stuffed somewhere into my voluminous purse, this man had an elegant leather holder and he held a monogrammed pen in his hand. He looked like the kind of man who didn't even handle paper money, as if that were a foreign concept, but dealt only in money via credit card. The chequebook looked unused, though his hand paused over it.

I blurted something out before I could even think. 'Fifty thousand dollars. For two hours.' Imagine earning my annual salary in just two hours! It was the first number that leaped to mind, but no sooner had I spoken the number aloud than the stranger was scrawling it across the rectangle on the light-blue paper, making it out to 'Cash'. 'Here, since I don't know your name yet,' he said, ripping it off and pressing it into my palm. 'I'm not even going to ask your name because I'm sure you'll just make one up. Oh, and I'm good for it,' he said, holding my hand as if to caress the dollars into my skin. When I glanced down at the cheque, I gasped, suddenly sure he was more than good for it. He wasn't exactly famous, but he appeared in the business pages often enough, and since that was the section I copyedited at the paper, I recognised Clay Barker, this titan of the high fashion industry.

'This is crazy,' I said, but didn't let go of the cheque. 'Maya,' I added, more softly. The man sitting next to us was agog, but scooted slightly away, knowing that whatever game we were now playing, he couldn't compete.

'Perhaps,' he conceded, 'but I've done far crazier things in my day.' News headlines started to flash in my mind, stories about sex, drugs, strippers, trashed hotel rooms; he came from a wealthy family and before he'd decided to take over their business, he'd spent time sowing plenty of very expensive wild oats. 'Well? I have a room down the block, at the hotel.' Of course, he knew I'd know he meant the $600-a-night brand-new luxury hotel that had just opened, and of course he had a room there. He said it like everyone did.

He had to realise that a girl like me, a news junkie,

would know who he was, but so would any other woman here. He didn't have to buy me, or anyone, unless he wanted to, and that thought made me wet. He wasn't just trying to win me away from the loser at the bar, but to prove something. He didn't ask a thing about me before forking over that cash, like whether I did anal or liked facials or got high (for the record: once in a while, yes, and only with high-quality pot). He didn't need to know anything about me besides what was right in front of him, and wasn't offering up any other information about himself, either. It was take it or leave it, and as quickly as he'd whipped out his chequebook, I smiled back at him. 'Let's go.' I didn't bother knocking back the rest of my drink, like I normally would have, since surely they had finer ones at his hotel. I just picked up my bag, tucked the cheque into the zippered compartment inside, and held out my arm before I I could regret it.

'Beautiful night, isn't it?' he asked as we walked, while I was bursting with questions. Should I go cash the cheque immediately and make sure it doesn't bounce? Does he proposition women like this all the time? What's the most he's spent on a call girl? Did this make me a hooker? What did he want to do first? All of them seemed uncouth to even think about. Would a real hooker think these things? Did that even matter because I wasn't one?

I mentally paused even as I kept walking arm in arm

with him, using my yoga training to centre my mind, and asked myself the most important question of all: did I want to go back to his hotel room? Did I want to offer myself up to him on a figurative silver platter, my body his for being the highest bidder? What was the true difference between a hundred dollars and what he'd offered me? The tingling rush of arousal in my pussy told me everything I needed to know. The money was like the icing on the cake, but it was the bold gesture, the way he'd swooped in and charmed me, without the arrogance of assuming that simply because he wielded a big chequebook I'd bow down before him. He'd seemed 90 per cent sure I'd say yes, but it was that other 10 per cent that made me want him.

'Penny for your thoughts?' he asked as we stopped at a red light.

'Just a penny? No longer a big spender?'

'Well, what would you like instead?' he asked, his gaze piercing me as suddenly the lights and commotion around us slipped away. I stared into his eyes and I was the one who leaned forward for a kiss. It was a soft kiss – at first. We pressed our lips together in greeting, in acknowledgment, in anticipation. This wasn't about the money, or even the power; yes, Clay had bought me, but clearly he didn't want me simply because he 'owned' me or because I 'owed' him. He wanted me because I was a woman, because, right now, he sensed something brewing between us that wasn't going to go away even if I ripped up the cheque.

That made me hot; I'd always fantasised about sex with a stranger, but stopped myself before it went that far. Flirting, yes, making out, sure, even a little groping, but some nagging part of my mind had stepped in before I ever went back to a stranger's apartment – or hotel room. First-date sex I'd had plenty of, but there's a lot more you can tell about a person after a two-hour dinner than a twenty-minute drink. So this was new for me on several levels, including the intense heat coursing through my body, from where his tongue met mine on down. Clay Barker knew how to kiss, and when he felt me melt against him, felt me surrender to him just enough for him to take control, he did, winding his hands through my hair and gripping it tightly enough to make me gasp. One hand moved to cup my ass and draw me closer, right there on the street, where anyone could see.

I loved the way his body felt so close to mine, and I also loved that everyone could see us. I wondered what they'd think if they knew I was getting paid $50,000 for this. Would they wonder if I was worth it? Would they want to try me for themselves? Then Clay's lips pulled me back completely into his embrace. 'Maya, Maya, Maya. I don't deserve you.' How could he know whether or not that was true when we'd barely said five sentences to each other? I didn't interrupt.

'What made you say yes?' he continued, tracing my cheek.

'I don't know,' I said honestly. 'I'm really not someone who's usually swayed by money. I mean, I do OK, I get by, and I'm happy with that. I can go out with my friends and indulge in drinks and dinners and the occasional fancy dress but mostly what I want are art supplies. My day job is the opposite of artistic, but it pays for my other love. Sure, fifty grand can buy a lot of art supplies but the truth is, I was intrigued. I wanted to know why a man would offer up so much money without even asking me what I'm into, what I'm like, what I'll do.'

'OK. I'm asking now. What are you into? What are you like? What will you do?'

I blushed as I let the questions wash over me. I'm into, well, slightly deviant things. I like to be tied up. Spanked and slapped – on my pussy, my ass, my tits, anywhere, really. Choked. Ordered around. Verbally degraded. Tickled, even though I have more of a love/hate relationship with that. Painful sensations and being put in my place. But I'd never told a stranger that. I'd only told two lovers, one of whom got it, one of whom didn't. I keep my kinks fairly close to the vest, or low-cut blouse, as it were.

Somehow, though, this whole episode, in all its heightened surreal nature, made me want to tell him everything. Not half the story, not a verbal gambit to see if he'd pounce on it, not what I thought he might want to hear. I had tried all those things in the past and while sometimes I'd wound up with some beautiful bruises, with my breath catching in my throat, with my body alive with the thrill of submission, it had never gone as far as I'd wanted. It had never gone all the way. I'd always held something, some vital part of myself, back, waiting for the moment to be right, and it never was, not exactly. This moment, maybe because of the money, maybe because I had nothing to prove – who cared if he liked me when this was done? – felt safe.

'I'm into spanking. Slapping. Choking. Kinky stuff. I'm the kind of girl who likes to please; I get off on it. I get very, very wet when I get down on my knees and if you put a cock in my mouth, well, I could stay there all night. I like to cry. I like to go somewhere else entirely, but be grounded right here while I'm being used. I like to be a little scared, a little nervous. I like for the guy to be in charge and to own that. To guide me. To use me completely for his own pleasure.' I was trembling by that point, the tears already waiting to be unleashed, my cunt suddenly painfully tight as the light turned from red to green and back again several times while I told Clay everything I could think of.

The words poured out of me, yet rather than feeling nervous, I felt calm, because I could see in Clay's eyes that he wasn't just listening passively, wasn't just filing away my words for in-the-near-future reference, but he fully got it – and liked it. 'Well, well, well,' he said, raising an eyebrow. 'If I were a betting man I'd say that we should head to Atlantic City, because those are all things I like to do to pretty girls like you. But a man in my position can't be too careful; I'm sure you know how easily a thing like this –' he gestured at me, running his fingers along my side from my ribs to my waist '– could get in the papers. And I don't think you want anyone to know that about you, do you, Maya? Anyone but me?'

We'd veered into dangerous territory, the leap from awkward to intimate jumped in mere moments. Suddenly it was as if he could've demanded *I* pay *him* $50,000 and I'd have done so in a heartbeat. It sounds crazy, in a way, but it didn't to me. I've always been a leap-before-I-look kind of girl, the one who follows her heart, or her pussy, occasionally both working in concert, far more than her head. What was even crazier was that as he said it, he made it true. Just as some guys can walk into a strip club and be instantly mesmerised by a certain girl, maybe because of the way she smiles at him, the way her lips glisten, the size of her breasts, the promise contained within her sweat-slick, shiny body, making him forget that they're in an alternate reality, I too chose to sustain disbelief. Well, 'chose' makes it sound like I had, well, a choice. I didn't, not really.

I was standing in the street, dripping wet, wishing

he'd grab me and shove me down onto the dirty sidewalk. This wasn't about the money, though we both knew he couldn't rescind the offer. The money was simply the gateway to our real purpose, a calling card a man like Clay used the way other men used pick-up lines or killer smiles. Clay took my arm and pinched the inside of it, about halfway between my wrist and my elbow. He held my flesh until I looked up from where our skin touched into his eyes. If he'd grabbed my ass, tried to spank me in the street, copped a feel, anything clichéd or ridiculous like that, I might've walked away. But what he did told me that he knew he could have me any way he liked. He could pinch any part of me and I'd respond with need.

But he only pinched that part, then settled his hand on my arm as we walked. He hummed to himself, almost as if I wasn't there, yet I was sure he was just as aware of our being together as I was, of this unexpected journey we were about to take. The more we walked, the more focused I became on the heat of his fingers warming my arm. My questions about his usual MO for picking up girls melted into fantasies of what I wanted him to do to me.

And then suddenly we arrived, and my sense that this was just a date dissipated as I walked in on his arm and he was greeted by name by three staff members. They knew him, and therefore clearly knew I hadn't been with him on his previous entrances. Maybe he'd brought other

11

women, but not me. It was two in the morning; I could only be either easy or a whore – or, most accurately, both.

We didn't linger, but I felt their eyes staring, trying to figure out if I was a one-night stand or something more. I wasn't sure what I wanted them to think of me, exactly, but I couldn't deny that the scrutiny made me wet. Clay's hand on my back led me towards the elevators, and soon we were paired with a couple who I was sure were, in fact, escort and client. She was young, with full, ripe lips and flawless skin, her curvy body crammed into a skin-tight black dress that barely kept her boobs inside. He was at least thirty years her senior, balding, while she was blonde, delicate and beautiful. She giggled and clung to him tighter, and I squeezed Clay's hand. Was I any different, or was that just wishful thinking?

We got off first, and he took my hand and held it up to his lips. 'Listen, if you want to back out now, I under-stand. I don't want you to do anything you don't want to. I'll even let you keep the cheque. But if you do come back with me, I'm going to make you earn it, Maya, every last dollar.' His voice got more ragged towards the end, and he backed me up against the wall so I could feel how hard he was. I looked into his eyes and swore I saw more than just lust.

'I'll come,' I said, and no sooner were the words out of my mouth than his hand was clutching my hair tightly, pulling my head back as he sank his teeth into my neck.

I could tell he was making a hickey, but I didn't care. I was so wet, so hungry for him.

We made our way to his room and as he sank the key card into the hole, he said, 'On your knees. You're going to crawl into that room like the whore you are.' I did it instantly, trembling with excitement. What did I care if anyone saw me? I no longer felt like myself, but a girl following his commands, ones I'd been waiting to hear for a long, long time. I crawled into the room, well aware of my ass being on full display. 'Keep going,' he said, nudging me gently with his foot as the door slammed shut behind us. He turned the lock.

'Lift up that skirt for me, and pull down your panties,' Clay instructed me. I was so wet my pussy almost hurt, and I hoped desperately that he was going to fuck me, or at least put his fingers, or really, at that point, anything, inside me. I pulled my skirt up over my hips and slid my panties down to mid-thigh, spreading my legs as far as possible. He leaned down and ran two fingers along my slit, pressing them against my sex but not entering me. 'So wet, that's what I like to feel. Get up and bend over the bed,' he said, and I did, stumbling a little in my heels. He peeled my panties off and pressed my thighs apart, rewarding me with another stroking of my pussy. 'I think you're going to like what I'm about to do, Maya, very, very much, so much that I have a feeling you might be tempted to scream, and while you probably have a beautiful scream, I don't want to be interrupted. So I'm going to shove these nice, wet panties in your mouth. If something is too much, I want you to kick off your left shoe. Do you understand?'

He turned me over onto my back and placed his hand around my neck, staring deep into my eyes. He looked almost kind even as he told me he wanted to gag me. 'If I had a real gag, I'd love to shove it between these pretty lips,' he said, before pinching them together. 'But this will have to do, until I take it out so I can put my cock there.' All that did was make me want his cock in my mouth even more than I wanted it in my pussy. 'Are you ready for your spanking, Maya? Because once I start, I'm not going to stop until I'm ready to fuck you or you kick off your shoe.'

'Yes, Clay, I'm ready.' He shoved the panties in my mouth, and I shut my eyes to focus on breathing through my nose. He turned me over onto my stomach once again. My arms were out towards my sides, though suddenly I wished I were totally naked, with my arms bound above my head. I didn't want to be tempted to try to cover myself, yet I knew that was part of my job – to be still, to force my hands to stay in place, to take his blows without trying to control them.

He didn't start with the spanking, though. Instead he played with my pussy a little more, inserting a finger just enough to tease, but not enough to even come close to getting me off. Then his wet finger pulled out and stroked my asshole, easily easing inside. 'What a sweet hole you have here, Maya. I might have to fuck you here instead of that very wet pussy of yours.' I was glad the panties were in my mouth, because I wasn't sure if I wanted to protest or agree. The truth was I wanted him in all my holes. He toyed with my ass for another minute or so before pulling out, pressing one hand on the small of my back and striking my right ass cheek hard, followed by an equally strong blow to the left one.

The heat of the smacks worked its way through me, and was quickly followed by more. He hit me right where I like it, striking the padded curves in a way that sent shock waves through my pussy. He was grunting, so I knew he was giving it his all, and he sustained a steady pace. The heat and pain and arousal mixed together until all I could feel was one big sensation blazing through me. Then he turned me over onto my back, and lifted my legs into the air, bringing my arms up to the backs of my thighs. 'Hold yourself open for me, my little whore,' he said, then let his hand land directly on my pussy. If my mouth hadn't been full, I'd have told him, 'Yes, yes,' because it felt so fucking good, but all I did was clutch my thighs tightly, feeling the strain there as I held myself open for him. 'You like that, don't you? I can tell you're getting wet for me,' he said, his voice just loud enough to let me know he wasn't only talking to himself.

'I guess it's a good thing I bought some toys today, in case I met a beautiful slut like you who wanted me to hurt her. Keep those legs open for me, Maya,' he said, and I did, even spreading my legs a little bit more, even though the strain of the position was harder to maintain. I shuddered when he walked back with a small strip of leather, the kind I'd seen but never felt against my skin. He ripped my blouse so the buttons went flying, then rubbed the edge of the toy against each hardened nipple, before raining the leather right against my nipples while I watched. The sound of the leather hitting my skin seemed loud in the otherwise quiet room, and he kept going. My nipples blazed with pain, the kind that went directly to my pussy. I wondered if it were possible for me to ejaculate just from him hitting me like that.

When my nipples were duly chastened, he moved on to my pussy, slapping gently against it, which only made my lips more engorged. Then he was truly slapping me there, the blows making me tremble. For a second, I wondered if I should toss my shoe on the floor, kick my leg out and put a stop to this, because the pain was so intense, but then that initial sting would abate and the sweet buzz would settle deep into my core. I hated it, but I loved it, and ultimately I wanted him to keep going more than I wanted him to stop. Clay slapped the leather against my inner thighs, then back to my pussy a few more times before tossing the toy on the bed and climbing up next to me.

He pulled the panties out of my mouth and leaned down to kiss me. His tongue claimed my mouth and made me even wetter. I thought about that line in *Pretty Woman*, where Julia Roberts says she doesn't kiss on the mouth, and decided that she'd been missing out. This was one of the best kisses of my life, and not because I was getting paid. Clay pulled away, leaving me panting, aching for his tongue, and his cock. 'Look at me, Maya. I have something for you.' I hadn't realised I'd shut my eyes until I opened them to see his face, intense, serious, stern. He brought his hand up and tapped my cheek, making me shudder. He slapped it lightly and I squirmed, and then he did it again, hard. 'Struggle for me, Maya. I want to have to subdue you. I want to have to hold you down while I spread those pretty legs and force my cock between them. Are you going to do that for me, Maya?' He paused and lifted himself off me, genuinely waiting for an answer. He wanted to make sure that was my fantasy, too.

'Yes, Clay, yes,' I said. I'd never spoken about my rape fantasies, because how do you bring something like that up, how do you ask for the one thing you're never supposed to? Yet he'd seen it in me, or maybe just in himself, and here he was, offering it to me. 'Yes,' I said again, suddenly eager for what was about to happen.

17

He got up again and stripped, then took out a roll of silver duct tape. I scrambled to get up and he pounced on me.

'No screaming,' he said, his voice going darker, deeper. 'You know you can't get away, sweet girl, so don't even think about trying. I have a friend down at the bar I can call to hold you down for me, if I need to. He won't be as nice as I am.' He straddled my chest, his hard cock pressing into me, and when I tried to press him off, I couldn't budge him. 'Now where should I start with this tape? I want those pretty lips ready for my cock, so I think I'll do your arms.' When he lifted his hand from my mouth, I moaned, trying to twist away from him, but he was big and heavy and I couldn't, even though each attempt to escape made me wetter. The sticky side of the tape pressed against my wrists until he had them coiled together.

'Where next, my sweet? I could put this anywhere I want,' he said, caressing my cheek with the tape, then rolling it between my breasts and along my stomach before easing it between my legs. I squirmed as I realised he could place the tape right there, along my wetness. I was utterly at his mercy, and that made me shiver. He'd bought far more than I'd bargained for back at the bar.

'Oh, does that make you excited?' he asked, resting the tape on my stomach as he pressed his fingers into my cunt. 'You want me to put the tape here? But what about me doing this?' He slapped my slit and I spread my legs wider, and he did it again. 'Yeah, that would be a shame to cover up these slick, beautiful lips,' he said as he tugged on one of them. Just as I was getting into his actions, he stopped and proceeded to place tape over my nipples. I moaned, already imagining what it would feel like coming off.

'Oh God, Maya, you are so fucking hot.' He was breaking his dominant mode, which made me smile a little, until he leaned down and bit my stomach, a random location but one that made me moan, his mouth so close to my pussy. He did, actually, ease his head down to lap at me for a few seconds, again so brief they were more torture than anything else. 'I'm wasting my precious time here when I should be making sure I get my money's worth of this tight pussy.'

I'd almost forgotten for a few seconds exactly why we were there, or, more accurately, how we'd come to be there, because the money was no longer why I was there. He could've ripped up the cheque and I'd have stayed exactly where I was, legs spread, panting, eager for him to slide his now condom-covered cock inside me, which is exactly what he did. No sooner was he fully inside me than he ripped the tape off my nipples. The pain was intense and immediate, and he didn't try to soothe me, but instead captured a nipple between his lips and sucked and bit while pinching the other. I squirmed, and he moved on to tickle me, before gently placing his hand over my mouth.

'So beautiful, Maya … how did I find you?' he asked, the words soft compared to the way he was pounding me. I came like that, my muffled cries against his hand, my cunt unleashing an orgasm it seemed I'd spent a lifetime building.

He speared me over and over, until I was limp, still feeling every sensation but also looking down at myself, my true self, a girl who'd whored herself out to the highest bidder and been rewarded with a man whose lifetime of knowledge of women was being put to use on me. An image of him beating another girl, a beautiful young thing with a gag in her mouth and tears in her eyes, ones I simply knew were tears of joy, made me come again, and Clay held my bound hands down against the bed with one hand while he pulled his dick out with the other, removed the condom in the same motion, and sprayed me all over with his come.

Right before I fell asleep, I glanced at the clock. Technically, Clay had two minutes to spare.

* * *

Later, as we lay in his bed, well past my allotted two hours, his lips curved up into a grin. 'I'd have gone much higher, you know. I just had a feeling you'd be worth it.'

'And you could've had me at a bargain price.' It was true, though I wasn't about to rip up the cheque.

'Maybe I can put you on retainer. Forever.' His eyes again speared me with a look of such intensity I was almost scared, but I breathed deeply and then leaned back, sticking out my hand.

'You've got a deal.'

I thought he'd meant a monthly retainer, another string of numbers with long strings of zeros behind them, and he did – but as his wife, complete with blinged-out diamond ring. Sometimes the best offer pays off in ways you can never predict. I stroked his hair as I reached for the phone to call room service, then hung up. 'Let's go out instead,' I said, looking forward to letting him show me off, and vice versa. Still, I hoped I'd someday get another chance to walk into a hotel with him and play the role of woman of the night, second only to being her.

The Three Rules for Selling Sex
Lisette Ashton

1. Always get the money up front.

2. Always have sex under an assumed name.

3. Be a whore – not a slut.

* * *

1. Always get the money up front.

You're going to think I'm an absolute whore for saying this but money is the thing that always turns me on. I think money is the thing that separates whores like me from those sluts who will do anything to please the guy they're with.

It's been this way ever since I started seeing Peter.

As soon as I feel money in my fingers, I enjoy a minor thrill of arousal. It's as though there's a money sensor in my fingertips, and that sensor triggers a reaction in my pussy. Push a five or a ten into my hand and the inner muscles of my sex clench as though they're ready to feel something slide inside my wetness. Push a twenty into my hand and I will hold my breath whilst my pulse quickens.

I have genuinely climaxed whilst holding two fifty-pound notes.

This is because I'm a whore – not a slut. There's a difference.

In some ways my instantaneous arousal is an embarrassing response that extends beyond my work as a whore. Recently, for a single week, I stopped working in the sex industry and took a conventional job, working as a cleaner in a hotel. When the duty manager paid me on the first Friday evening, I came close to fucking him simply out of habit.

We were in a hotel. It was a hotel where I'd occasionally worked in the past as a call girl. (Coincidentally, it was the first hotel where I screwed Peter.) The duty manager was thrusting a wad of notes into my hand. And the feel of the money in my fingers was enough to give me the same thrill I got from being paid up front by a client.

Three fifties, two twenties and a ten.

I could have climaxed on the spot. He was paying me enough for anal.

I disappeared to one of the hotel's rooms and satisfied the appetite awoken by the Pavlovian response of holding notes in my sweaty hand. I rubbed myself to a furious, frenzied climax whilst sniffing the dirty money. An hour later I quit the cleaning job and returned to my more lucrative calling of being a call girl. I can honestly say I haven't looked back.

Talking about money gives me a thrill.

It's foreplay for me because conversations about money always precede a session of slow, sultry sex. It's more exciting than cunnilingus. It's more arousing than a pornographic movie.

My panties get wet whenever the client says to me, 'How much?'

I don't mean my panties get *sopping* wet. I'm not going to pretend that I'm constantly horny and desperate for cock. But the subject of money turns me on in conversation. The subject gives me a chance to tease and flirt and take control of the exchange.

'How much for what?' I ask.

I always lower my voice to a husky whisper. It adds to the illusion that our transaction is something discreet, unusual and extraordinary, rather than something that's likely happening in a hundred or more different hotel rooms within a single square mile of where we stand.

'What services do you offer?' he asks.

This is the point where my nipples harden. The skin tightens as the buds of flesh fill with blood. The sensitivity radiates through the shrinking confines of my bra. The client usually discusses sex in terms of euphemisms. He will ask about the *services* I provide, as though I'm going to defrost his freezer or offer to rewire his house. It's very rare that the client will be forthright enough to say: 'How much for a blow job? How much for straight sex? How much for anal?'

To some extent, I'm pleased about that.

Conversations without euphemism tend to strip away the mystery of the sex act and make the whole encounter seem more like a tawdry and vulgar transaction. When we talk in euphemisms it's as though I'm sharing some sort of telepathy with the client. We're talking about *costs* and *services* and *extras*, and we're meaning my mouth around his cock, or half an hour with our sweaty naked bodies writhing together, or his length sliding into the depths of my ass.

'The cost depends on what you want. Half an hour of my time will cost you a straight hundred. It's another hundred for each part of a half-hour after that. If you want anything kinky then I might have to charge extra.'

I always meet the client's eye when I say the word 'kinky'.

If I can give a suggestive smile too it helps build

rapport. And, if the client happens to have a kink that I haven't tried before, it's convenient for me to get paid for my experimentation.

It was through the suggestiveness of a client that I discovered the pleasures of wielding a whip. It was through one customer's need to administer a 'kinky' spanking that I found out how pleasurable it is to have my buttocks turned warm crimson by the slap of a large manly hand.

And so, after I've mentioned the word 'kinky' I give the client a moment to recall if he has any vices he'd like to explore. It's another of those moments that makes me hold my breath. I'm aware I could be on the verge of encountering another life-changing experience. And, if the client's suggestion sounds too depraved for my simple tastes, I can always ask for extra money to compensate me for the experience.

If he thinks it's my first time, the client is always happy to pay extra.

I always talk about *time* when I'm making negotiations with a client. I never talk about specific acts if I can avoid such details. But, whilst I'm talking about the cost of my time, I think about the image of my bare body pressed against the naked body of the client. I try to send him a mental picture of my mouth against his and our bare flesh sliding smoothly and rhythmically together.

I'm not sure whether or not that particular trick works.

26

But I've rarely been turned down once I've started discussing terms.

Most of the time I'm paid in twenties.

Once I've rubbed the money between my fingertips – resisting the urge to smell the musk of those notes that have been passed from hand to hand and used to secure countless transactions before – I'm just about ready to begin. And I say it to myself like a mantra: always get the money up front.

I have to get the money up front because I'm not a slut. I'm a whore.

* * *

2. Always have sex under an assumed name.

'What do I call you?'

It's a common enough question. And it's one to which I always try to avoid giving an honest answer.

'Call me Magenta.'

'That's not your real name.'

'It's real enough for the moment, isn't it?'

My working name is Magenta. If the client presses me to know what my real name is, I tell him it's Maggie. Usually the client is happy to call me Magenta and he calls me that for the remainder of his time with me. When the client calls me Maggie it seems to let him believe he's having sex with someone other than the persona I usually play in a stranger's hotel room.

I don't mind.

Whatever gives him the satisfaction he craves. If it makes the client consider giving me a tip afterwards then he can call me anything he likes. Whatever it takes to help fulfil his fantasy.

And that's really what the job is all about.

From the moment the cash is safely stuffed into my purse, I allow myself to be the subject of the client's fantasy. My smile grows broader. I give in to the thrill of electric excitement that tightens the air. And I start to tease myself out of the clothes I'm wearing.

Sometimes the client expects a striptease.

There are other times when the client is happy for me to screw him whilst I'm fully clothed, with just my skirt hitched up to expose the tops of my stockings and the crotch of my thong wrenched to one side so he can slide his sheathed erection into the wetness of my hole. But most times the client is curiously satisfied to watch me undress whilst he comes to accept that we're about to fuck.

It's not an automatic understanding. The client seldom assumes that sex is going to go ahead until I start to unbutton my blouse. And then you can see the lascivious smile of desire flicker in his eyes. He stares appreciatively at Magenta's body knowing he's paid for her for the pleasure of her company over the next thirty minutes.

And that thought really does make me wet.

The first time I had sex for money was back in college. There was a guy called Peter and I'd fancied him for an age. From the first day I'd been studying alongside him I'd wanted him. And, even though it would have been the reprehensible behaviour of a slut, I would have happily fucked him for free. More than that, I would have paid him if I'd thought he would have fucked me for the money.

But Peter was a rich college boy with no need for the little money I could have scraped together. He was tall and dark and boyishly good-looking. A wealthy relative had left him an endowment that made him seem like a lottery winner on the campus. And, to my frustration, Peter and I had fallen into the trap of being platonic best friends rather than passionate lovers.

I'd spend study nights round at his apartment and he'd provide pizza and bottles of cheap lager. I kept promising myself that I'd make a move but it never seemed like the right time. It wasn't until there came a night when we were both amicably drunk that I plucked up the courage to say something bold.

We'd been watching an old movie on TV: *Pretty Woman*. It's the film where Julia Roberts plays a whore to Richard Gere's client. As sex was a main topic throughout the film, I took the opportunity to ask Peter if he'd ever paid for sex.

He laughed. It was a strong sound that made me yearn

for him. Swigging from his bottle he said, 'I've never paid for sex. What about you?'

I shook my head. I had expected to catch myself blushing but I seemed beyond embarrassment. 'Women don't pay for sex,' I reminded him. 'Women are the ones who get paid.'

He considered this and then nodded as though my point made sense. 'Then I'll rephrase the question. Have you ever been paid to have sex?'

I studied him levelly. 'Are you offering?'

He laughed again. This time I saw it was bashful laughter. He clearly sensed we were overstepping the boundaries of our platonic relationship. And, whilst that was something he had been trying to avoid, it was a barrier I was desperate to breach.

'Are you offering?' I repeated. 'I won't be offended if you try to put a price on the contents of my pants. You never know. It might be more affordable than you think.'

His cheeks were touched by twin spots of colour. It was quite endearing. 'I couldn't afford someone as classy as you.'

'Are you sure? Why don't you put some notes in my hand and see what happens?'

His mouth worked soundlessly for a moment. His eyes shone with a smile that made me desperate for him. And I could see that he was seriously considering my suggestion.

'Put some notes in my hand,' I urged, 'and I'll tell you what I'm prepared to do for that amount of money. There's only you and I in the flat this evening so I'm sure this conversation won't go any further.'

We were sitting in the kitchen of his apartment. It was surprisingly tidy, but that was only because Peter could afford for a cleaner to visit twice a week. A glass-topped table was between us and I watched him reach into the pockets of his jeans as he struggled to find cash.

His hands were shaking.

I wasn't entirely sure, but I thought it looked like he was already sporting a modest erection that thrust at the zipper of his jeans.

In that moment the dynamics of our relationship changed.

We'd been platonic friends before. Now, Peter saw me as someone sexual. More than that, if he produced enough notes, he would see me as someone sexual that he could possess. The thought melted my loins. All that was needed was for me to maintain my integrity and be a whore – not a slut.

Peter deserved more than a mere slut.

'Here,' he said quickly. He pulled out a five-pound note and put it in my upturned palm.

I sneered. 'I wouldn't even look at your cock for that much. I certainly wouldn't do anything sexual for a fiver.'

But, even as I said the words, there was a tremor in my voice. And I was sure that Peter had heard as much.

31

To cover my embarrassment, I lifted the note to my nostrils and pretended to study it closely.

That was when the smell first hit me.

There is a distinctive scent to a five-pound note. It smells of sex. It reminds me of the musky scent I can catch on the gusset of my panties at the end of the day. It's a lingering aroma of arousal that taints each well-thumbed banknote. As I drank in the fragrance of the five-pound note that Peter had placed in my hand I found the intoxicating aroma had already started to make my pussy muscles clench.

Peter passed me a twenty.

He said nothing. There was only the brittle stiffness of a crisp note touching my palm. As the silence dragged on he eventually asked, 'What would you do for that?'

I yawned, feigning a boredom I had never felt in Peter's company. A boredom I could never feel. 'Double it,' I said idly, 'and I'll suck your cock.'

The words were strong enough to wrench the air from the room.

Peter swallowed. There was a moment when I thought I'd gone too far.

And then he was fumbling in his pockets trying to find more money.

I lowered my voice to a sultry whisper. 'Do you want to feel my lips around your cock?' I asked. 'I could suck you so hard for fifty pounds that you'd swear it was the best investment you ever made.'

Through the glass-topped table I could see the bulge at the front of his pants had grown considerably. Peter made no attempt to hide his arousal as he rummaged through his pockets in the search for more cash.

'That suh-sounds pretty guh-good,' he stammered.

'For one hundred you can slide your cock inside me,' I murmured. 'My pussy is so wet for you now I think I'd drown you with it.'

I shifted in my seat so that he noticed I was wearing a short tartan skirt. It was a short tartan skirt that was visible through the glass-topped table.

He went still.

I placed my hand on the hem of the skirt and began to draw it slowly upwards. Peter's eyes grew wider as the skirt moved higher. His mouth hung open and then he was drawing a tongue across his lips and swallowing with obvious, urgent need.

I couldn't stop myself from grinning.

His gaze was fixed on my thighs. The hem of the skirt had crept so high that, I knew, it would be possible for him to see the white cotton crotch of my panties. I wondered if the panties looked as moist as they felt. Talking about money, and threatening to suck Peter's cock, had made my inner muscles flow with fluid need for him. I could imagine the white centre panel of the panties was silvered with the dew from my eager sex.

I slipped the fingers of my right hand away from the hem of the skirt and brushed a fingernail against the gusset of my panties. The tickle of my own touch was almost enough to make me climax.

I snatched a staggered breath. And I held myself rigid for fear of suffering an orgasm before we'd properly done anything together.

Peter raised his gaze to study my eyes.

'A hundred pounds and you can slide your cock in here,' I told him. Without allowing myself to think about the action, I tugged the crotch of my panties to one side.

I was touched by the delightful chill of the kitchen's cold air against my exposed pussy lips. The thrill of that cool chill brought me close to exploding. I clenched the muscles of my thighs, trembling with the vibrant need I harboured for Peter. And I steeled my voice to sound cool, calm and unperturbed. 'Do you want this?' I asked.

'Oh! Yes.'

I stroked a finger against my sex. The lips parted immediately, as though they were urging him to hurry up and find the necessary money. I wasn't sure if it was the intensity of my imagination or a symptom of my arousal but I believed I could smell the piquant aroma of my need for him.

Peter began rummaging again through his pockets. He

34

pulled out another twenty and a ten. A third twenty fell onto the table. I thought it had fallen directly in the line of his view of my pussy and I was pleased that he pushed it to one side. He stood up to delve deeper and I noticed that the thrust of his excitement was shamelessly pressing at the front of his jeans. I barely noticed as he pulled out another pair of tens. And then a twenty. I was captivated by the sight of his denim-sheathed erection.

'That's more than a hundred,' I observed.

I was stroking my fingertip back and forth against the line of my labia. The flesh was maddeningly sensitive. The slippery wetness allowed my finger to glide easily against the bare flesh. Instead of touching myself I wanted to reach up and stroke the thick girth of his bulge.

'If you've got more than a hundred available perhaps we could do more?' I suggested.

'Such as?' Peter croaked.

I slid my finger into the wetness of my hole. The sensation was not devastating but it did send a long warm tingle throbbing deep through my sex. When I slipped the finger out, I stood up and touched it against Peter's lip.

He closed his eyes as though in an ecstasy of bliss.

'For two hundred pounds I'll let you take me up the ass.'

Peter groaned.

'For this much,' I began. I scooped up the money and

squeezed it in one fist. The sensation of the crumpled notes against my palm was a glorious spur to my excitement. I felt light-headed as I realised I was holding more than a hundred pounds of his money. I tossed the five-pound note back onto the table and held up the hundred pounds. 'For this much, I'll let you screw me for the next thirty minutes.'

'Are you serious, Ma–?'

I silenced his words with a kiss. 'When we're playing this game you can call me Magenta. If you don't want to call me Magenta you can call me Maggie. But you must never call me by my real name when we're having sex for money. Do you understand?'

He shrugged instantaneous acceptance of this request. I doubt he understood the condition. I'm still not sure I understand why I made the distinction. But the important thing was that Peter didn't question my demand.

'Whatever you want, *Magenta*.'

The name sounded strangely forced, and that added to my excitement. Peter was paying to have sex. He was going to screw someone called Magenta. And I was going to get to watch the experience and take the money afterwards.

My heart raced.

And then I was taking the initiative and pushing myself against him.

His hand went clumsily to my breast. I allowed him

to fumble against me for a moment and then I pushed him away. Unfastening the buttons for him, I opened my blouse and pulled my right breast free from the cup of the bra.

The nipple was stiff and sensitive to his touch.

And when Peter began to tease it between his fingertips, I came close to climaxing from the thrill of his caresses.

Our mouths met. He kissed with a slobbering need that would have been unappealing if he hadn't given me one hundred pounds. Because I could still smell traces of the money in my nostrils, his over-enthusiastic kisses were just another spur to my burgeoning excitement.

And, when he lowered his mouth to my nipple and began to suckle against me, I told him he was doing it very well. I patted the back of his head. And I stared at the money on the table with avid appreciation.

The sex was brutally swift.

I had a pack of condoms in my purse and I rolled one over his erection. He was thick and hard – almost pulsing to my touch as I slid the rubber down his shaft. I worried that I might squeeze the come from him if I rolled it too hard.

But Peter found a moment's inner strength and resisted the urge to climax long enough for me to drag him into his bedroom and straddle him on the bed.

'I can't believe you and I are doing this, Ma– Magenta.'

He'd almost called me by my name. His last-moment correction made me smile. And that was when I finally managed to slide his thick shaft between my sopping pussy lips. I don't think he'd fully filled me before my inner muscles were clenching and convulsing around him.

And, as soon as my orgasm had taken hold, I felt him thrash and pulse and climax as though he was retaliating.

I left him alone on the bed whilst I disposed of the condom and then went to retrieve my money. I counted it whilst I lay on the bed next to him. Four twenties and two tens. I'd also picked up the spare five pounds because I figured I'd earned the small bonus.

'Have you done this before?' he asked.

I shook my head. 'No.' I sniffed the money and, without thinking, added, 'But I'll be happy to do it again and again as long as you can find the funds.'

He nodded. 'But next time,' he said, 'I want to do this at a hotel so it's more convincing.'

I nodded agreement, inhaling the fragrance on the notes he'd given me. 'I can live with that,' I agreed. 'Although I might increase my prices for hotel work.'

He thought about this for a moment and then smiled. 'If I'm paying more money, I'll expect you to behave like a real slut.'

'No,' I said calmly. 'I'll never behave like a slut. Just a whore.'

He seemed puzzled by the distinction.

Rather than explaining, I kissed him. 'Let's negotiate money,' I purred. 'Then I'll tell you what you can expect when we're next in a hotel together.'

* * *

3. Be a whore – not a slut.

I still see Peter on a regular basis. He doesn't know it but I'm exclusively his. I keep increasing my prices for him because I need the money and he can afford it. Also, paying for it makes him appreciate what he's getting. And, whilst his demands are becoming more exciting and outrageous every time we get together, I'm determined to make him pay more for each new kink he introduces to our sex life. I'm keen to let him know that I'm his whore: not his slut. And one day I think he'll appreciate the difference.

A Red Carnation
Monica Belle

'Remember, I'll be wearing a red carnation.'

Gemma smiled. It was a wonderfully old-fashioned touch, and most things old-fashioned appealed to her, at least when it came to men. Too many were either pushy, or needy, or just plain crazy, but John had behaved like a gentleman from the start and as she got up from the computer she had crossed her fingers in hope that he might at last prove to be the right one. If so, she reflected, it was about time. John would be her twenty-first internet date. Of the previous twenty, twelve had been unsuitable for one reason or another, five had failed to turn up at all, and three had looked so awful that she'd sneaked away from the rendezvous instead of introducing herself.

Those last three had taught her an important lesson,

to always make sure that she could pick him out from a crowd but not vice versa. John seemed nice, gentlemanly but masculine too, with a touch of the paternal that gave her a pleasant sensation of weakness, but then she'd felt the same way about Ian. Online Ian had been suave, voluble and firm without ever going over the boundary, while his pictures had shown a tall, slim man in early middle age, with an intelligent face and a touch of grey at his temples. When she had arrived at the pub where they'd agreed to meet she'd found the same man, but in the sixty-year-old edition, with a bulbous red nose and no hair at all, while his hand had been on her knee and sneaking slowly up her skirt within five minutes of meeting.

She went to make coffee, her tummy still tight after her conversation with John and her mind racing for the possibilities he offered. It had been a long time, far too long, and for all her need for a gentle but firm seduction by a man under complete self-control she found her thoughts turning to more earthy matters: the feel of strong, masculine hands on her body, the sense of utter vulnerability once her legs were wide and his weight was on top of her and, most of all, the feel of a thick excited cock easing into her vagina. Back at the computer she logged on to her favourite social networking site in an effort to concentrate on something other than the sense of need in her head and between her thighs, but nobody she really wanted to talk to was online and she quickly gave up. She closed her eyes as she unfastened her jeans, speaking to herself as she slipped a hand down the front of her panties.

'You are a disgrace, Gemma, but never mind. One last time and then I'll have a man, with any luck. Please, God, let this be the one.'

* * *

The knot in Gemma's stomach had been growing tighter with every clack of the train's wheels. It had always been the same, with every date, her tension rising throughout the journey to reach a peak when the moment came to meet her man. Instead of fading, the sensation had been growing worse, and this time was no exception. What had begun as a fairly casual exercise after the break-up of her marriage had grown ever more desperate, her need ever greater, the disappointment of failure ever sharper. Still she was determined not to compromise, and to present herself as well as she possibly could. For John, and an evening out in the city centre, she had perfected her hair and make-up before slipping into a pair of lacy, figure-hugging panties, which left no trace of their presence beneath the indigo silk of her evening gown, along with sheer stockings and heels to match her dress. Even with a coat on over the top she was drawing glances, some merely curious but many admiring, which gave a much-needed boost to her confidence as she stepped from the train.

John had said he would be by the bookstall at the centre of the station concourse, and Gemma suffered a sharp pang of disappointment when she saw that nobody who could possibly have answered his description was there, with or without a red carnation. A glance at her watch showed that she still had nearly ten minutes to wait, but as she glanced around she saw him and the knot in her stomach grew painfully tight. He was near perfect, perhaps a few years older than she'd expected, with pepper-and-salt hair rather than brown, but he was tall, slim and carried himself with an almost military bearing. A well-cut suit in a reserved grey suggested both gentility and taste, while his choice of a tie to match the flower in his buttonhole seemed very orderly, just as she liked men to be. Better still, he had that slightly stern, uncompromising look that she liked in men, so much so that as she set off across the concourse her nipples had begun to stiffen against the silk of her dress.

'Hello, I'm Gemma. You must be John.'

His immediate reaction was a puzzled frown, but it lasted only an instant before he gave her a warm, open smile. 'Gemma? Hello, how are you? I'm very glad you made it. Shall we?'

He offered her his arm, a gesture she found irresistible,

and as he guided her from the station she was struggling to restrain her feelings of elation. Outside, he hailed a cab, which drew up immediately opposite them. The previous passenger got out, a slightly overweight, rather seedy-looking individual in a tatty brown suit with a drooping red carnation in the buttonhole. Gemma immediately found herself smiling for the potential mistake she might have made, knowing that if she had seen the man in the brown suit first she would have got straight back on the train.

As it was she was with John, the man of her dreams, and he seemed to know exactly what he was doing. There were no awkward moments, no embarrassed silences, no hesitant conversations as they tried to work out each other's preferences. He simply took the reins, instructing the cabbie where to go then opening a discussion on fine food and cookery. It was something they'd touched on while talking online, but Gemma was surprised at how much he knew, and at how easy she found it to defer to him. There was none of the irritation she so often felt with male conversation, while his easy charm but slightly stern manner made it hard to disagree.

The cab ride ended at one of the city's most exclusive hotels, and Gemma found herself being ushered into a magnificent dining room by polite but formal waiters in immaculate uniforms. She had expected a bistro, or some café in the French style at the very best, and found herself hoping that John didn't expect her to pay her share of the bill. From his manner it seemed unlikely. The menu was a large booklet of cream-coloured card decorated with a gold tassel and didn't show any prices at all, which suggested that if you needed to know how much the dishes cost then you couldn't afford them. John was indifferent, discussing the various delicacies on offer and consulting her on her own choices in order to allow him to select an appropriate wine.

Gemma found herself enthralled as the evening progressed, by the refinement of the setting, by John's manners and conversation, by his naturally dominant personality. Before long she knew that not only was she willing to go to bed with him, but that she would be unable to resist. She had always enjoyed the sensation of being protected and yet vulnerable to the very man who had granted her that protection, but never before had anybody made her feel so deliciously weak.

With the meal complete and the bill paid by John simply ordering the money be put on his account, Gemma gave no resistance whatsoever as she found herself being steered upstairs. He quite clearly had a room booked in advance, which implied that he'd assumed he would be taking her to bed even before they'd met, but what would have been an impossibly arrogant act in any other man seemed entirely natural with John. She was also slightly drunk and highly aroused, too far gone to worry about anything but her immediate needs.

The room was beautiful, furnished in pale yet rich shades of white and tan and gold, illuminated by a magnificent chandelier and furnished with several chairs and a huge four-poster bed. John guided her inside, closed the door and took her in his arms as she opened them to his embrace. He seemed a trifle surprised at the yielding passion of her kisses, but responded eagerly enough, their tongues entwined even as he manoeuvred her towards the bed. She felt fragile, almost limp, allowing him to manipulate her body as they sat down together on the bed, only to cry out in surprise as she was swiftly and skilfully turned down across his knee into a position that could mean only one thing. He was going to spank her, an intention he confirmed even as he tucked his arm under her tummy to hold her firmly in place.

'Now then, let's get your bottom warmed, shall we, young lady?'

Gemma's answer was a weak sob, because for all the appalling outrage of what was about to be done to her she felt unable to resist. It even felt right, in a way, to be put across his knee and have her bottom smacked, for all that it went against everything she'd been taught to believe about how a man should treat a woman. She did make an attempt to get up, telling herself that it was impossible to let such a thing happen to her, but John merely tightened his grip as he spoke once more.

'Now, now, let's not have any nonsense out of you,

miss. We both know you deserve this, and you're going to get it.'

Again Gemma tried to find her voice, outraged by the idea that she, or any woman, could possibly deserve to have a man spank her, and yet that very threat had made the melting, vulnerable feeling she enjoyed so much stronger still. She gave in, fighting her shame and resentment, telling herself that she was only prepared to surrender herself to the unspeakable indignity because she had no choice, but she knew it was a lie. As his hand settled across the seat of her dress she'd begun to sob, but in raw passion rather than the fear and misery she knew she ought to have felt.

John took no notice, but gave her bottom a thoughtful, almost proprietorial stroke, as if he owned her and had the right to do as he pleased. Then he began to spank, quite hard, each firm smack sending a stinging jolt through her body and making her gasp. Still she stayed down, her thoughts too muddled for resistance, hating every second of the pain and humiliation of what was happening but at the same time feeling it was exactly right. There was no denying the reaction of her body either, with her nipples stiff and her sex hot and damp, while with every smack of his hand to her bottom she found herself wanting to lift her hips as if for entry from behind.

He seemed to take her reaction for granted, or else he didn't care, holding her firmly in place while he spanked her, just as if he were dishing out a punishment to some-body he had real authority over, except in that he was openly enjoying himself with her bottom, pausing occasionally to stroke or squeeze her cheeks. There was something intensely intimate about his touch, intrusive even, and she knew she ought to feel that she was being molested, but she found herself incapable of resenting it, even when he began to tug up her dress.

'It's about time we had this up, don't you think?' he said, his voice stern but also mocking. 'If only to see what you have on underneath. Hmm, black and lacy, very pretty, but not white, Gemma. I expected white, and you know what that means, don't you?'

'No,' Gemma managed, shaking her head as she wondered how she could possibly have been expected to know what colour knickers he wanted her to wear.

'It means,' he told her as he tucked her dress up to leave the seat of her panties fully exposed, 'that they have to come down straight away, so that you get the rest of your spanking bare bottom. It seems almost a shame though, because you do have such a pretty bottom, and these do show you off beautifully. I almost hesitate to pull them down, almost ...'

As his voice trailed off he took hold of her panties and began to draw them slowly down. Gemma found her mouth coming wide as she was stripped behind, her feelings of indignation and shame warring with the irresistible sexual need building up inside her. If it was appallingly inappropriate to put a woman across the knee and spank her, then it was worse by far to take down her panties and do it on her bare bottom, especially when she was in a position that left every intimate secret of her body on show.

John plainly appreciated the view, taking her panties down to the level of her knees before once more starting to explore her bottom, his touch now more intimate and possessive than before. Gemma hung her head, sobbing with shame, as her cheeks were caressed and slapped, pinched and squeezed, then suddenly, without warning, hauled wide to show off her anus. Her mouth came wide in an inarticulate cry of emotion for what he'd done, but he merely laughed and went back to spanking her, now using the flat of his hand to strike up at her cheeks and make them wobble and spread.

'That's more like it,' he said happily, 'bare and bouncy, just the way a girl's bum should be, and my, do you have a beautiful bottom. I'm going to enjoy you, Gemma, I really am, but not until I've got you properly warm. Let's have those pretty boobies out then, shall we, and we'll get down to business? Lift up.'

Gemma found herself obeying, despite the feeling that she was being treated as a sex doll. As he began to tug her dress higher still, she had raised her body to make it easier for him, allowing her breasts to be stripped, then groped and smacked before he once again took a firm grip around her waist.

'Right, you little brat,' he snarled. 'Let's get you spanked.'

He'd lifted his hand as he spoke, and instantly brought it down, hard, across her bottom, so hard the smack knocked the breath from her body and left her gasping for air. Another followed, before she could manage to speak, and a third, the slaps now landing fast across her bouncing bottom cheeks to send her into a wriggling, squirming dance of pain, with her legs kicking in her lowered panties, her hair tossing wildly and her breasts jumping beneath her chest. It hurt far more than before, but after a few moments of anger and panic and helpless fear, her arousal had come back, stronger than ever. In just moments, she was sticking her bottom up, lost in an ecstasy she'd never imagined could exist, as she was spanked by the only man who'd ever had the courage to truly take charge of her. Then the pain was gone, with each and every smack across her bottom bringing only heat and pushing her arousal higher still. She began to beg him to do it harder and faster, and to fuck her, using crude, urgent words she'd scarcely dared to think before. With that the spanking stopped as suddenly as it had begun.

'You want it,' John panted, 'and you're going to get it.'

He had pulled Gemma around as he spoke, leaving her sitting hot-bottomed on the bed, but only for a moment before he jerked down his fly and whipped out a big, half-stiff cock and a set of heavy balls. She was dizzy with reaction and completely surrendered to her need and to his, unresisting as she was pulled roughly down into his lap and his cock stuffed into her mouth. His hand locked tight in her hair and she was being forced to suck, her head pulled up and down on his rapidly swelling erection, until she began to gag. Only then did he relent, keeping his grip in her hair but allowing her to set the pace. Gemma let his cock slip from her mouth as she swung around, deliberately climbing down and onto her knees on the carpeted floor.

'I thought you might like to get into that position,' he said. 'You're a natural, do you know that? A natural cock sucker, just like you're a natural to have your bottom spanked.'

Gemma didn't answer, her mouth full of cock once more as she began to work on his erection with a pleasure close to worship, kissing and licking in-between sessions with as much as she could get in her mouth. She sucked his balls and made a cunt of her lips, used the tip of her tongue to flick at the underside of his foreskin and her teeth to nibble gently at his shaft, every dirty little trick she'd ever heard of but never felt able to use, and all for her own pleasure as much as for his.

He took it all as if it was his due, but just when she thought he was sure to come and give her a welcome mouthful of hot spunk, he took her under the arms and pulled her up onto his body. She went, unresisting save for a faint flicker of resentment for not being asked, as he lifted her body onto his straining cock. His helmet pushed to her hole, the mouth of her cunt opened to accept him and it was too late anyway, her body filled with cock for the first time in far, far too long. She was squirming her bottom into his lap on the instant, lost in ecstasy, as she sat high to show off her breasts for him with her hands tangled in her hair, then lower, to let him suck on the stiff buds of her nipples and he pushed himself up and down inside her.

For a brief moment Gemma felt as if they were making love more or less as she was used to, and with that came an unexpected stab of disappointment. That vanished as his big hands clasped her waist and she was thrown down on the bed and mounted, her thighs high and wide to receive him as he thrust into her, now on top and once more firmly in charge. The fucking was fast and furious, with his cock pumping hard into her open cunt and his balls slapping on her smacked bottom cheeks, bringing her up to the edge of orgasm before he stopped and pulled out once more.

Gemma gave a groan of disappointment that turned into a squeak as she was grabbed once more and flipped over, now on her knees, a position even more vulnerable and receptive than before. His cock went back up, deep inside her, and he began to thrust again, as his hands found the cheeks of her bottom, spreading them to deliberately show off her anus and the junction of his erection and her cunt. Again she felt a faint stab of resentment for the way he was using her without the slightest reserve or consideration for her modesty, but she was too far gone to really care, let alone resist. Only when he pulled free, took hold of his cock and pressed it to her anus did she find her voice.

'John, no, please! That's too dirty.'

'Let's not have any of that nonsense, you apple-bottomed little slut,' he answered, and he began to rub the head of his cock on her anus.

Gemma responded with a low moan. There was no denying how good it felt, or the awful and secret craving she'd always fought against, to have her bottom hole penetrated, and yet everything she'd ever been taught resisted the act as too degrading, too submissive, something no self-respecting woman should ever do, only dirty girls with no self-respect, porn stars and whores.

'John, I don't ...'

He slapped her bottom, a single firm smack of admonishment, then he dipped his cock back into the open, wet cavity of her cunt. Gemma sighed as she felt herself fill once more, only to have him extract his erection and paint her juice over her anus. A push and she felt her ring start to spread, making her gasp in shock, and then again in pain as the delicious tight feeling turned to a bruising ache. Again John dipped his cock into her cunt and again he painted her anus with juice to help her open up, an act so filthy and so intimate Gemma could barely believe it was she who was allowing it to be done.

'Just relax,' he urged. 'It'll go. You can't be a virgin anyway, surely not?'

Gemma twisted around. 'I … of course I am, up there … up my bottom!'

'You are?' John sighed. 'Oh bliss!'

'I'd never been spanked before, either,' Gemma told him, her voice low and sulky. 'Do go on then, you might as well … you do make me want it.'

John gave a pleased purr at her words and pushed once more. This time his cock went in, spreading Gemma's bottom hole out around his helmet. Now buggered, the last of her reserve gave way. She took it, grunting and clutching at the bedclothes, begging him to push it deeper up and cursing him for the way he had treated her, until at last he was all the way in and, as he began to push, his balls slapped against her empty cunt. With that she put her face in the bed covers to sob out her feelings, as she gave in to the dark, dirty needs she'd always held back.

No longer able to speak, she knew she was going to come, her sole concern that she got there first, as her buggering grew harder and faster. She screamed out her passion and squirmed her bottom into his lap, against ever harder thrusts until at last they came together, John with a single harsh grunt and Gemma with a scream that echoed every moment of her past frustration and reserve, now gone in one perfect moment.

* * *

Gemma woke to bright sunlight and cool air on one leg where the covers had slipped off. It took her a moment to remember where she was and another to realise that she was alone in bed. She sat up, the sheet clutched to her naked chest, but there was no sign of John and the only sound was the faint hum of a vacuum cleaner mixed with the traffic outside. Her dress was on a chair by the window, neatly folded, her pretty black panties laid out on top and on top of them a small pile of what she saw were twenty-pound notes. Puzzled, she climbed from the bed and padded across to pick up the notes and count them, all the while with an awful suspicion growing in her head. A piece of paper fluttered out from among the notes and she picked it up. She read the words written in a firm flowing hand and her mouth came slowly open in horror:

'Dear Gemma, Got to go, but's here's the money. You were great, the best escort I've had in years, especially the way you took your spanking as if you really didn't like it, and how you pretended to be a virgin when I put it up your bum. I'll definitely be booking you again! John.'

Sorry, Right Number
Rose de Fer

Juliet was dabbing at her smeared mascara and wondering how the hell she could leave the restaurant with any kind of dignity when her phone bleeped. She was grateful for the distraction, sure that absolutely everyone was still staring at her over their tiramisu. It had been an ugly scene, one that Matt had contrived to have in public, incorrectly assuming that it would shield him from any drama.

Someone from 'number withheld' had sent her a text. Probably one of Matt's friends, eager to 'console' the now single Juliet. She thumbed the button and read the message: '8.15 Montefiore Hotel room 903, bdsm slave, £1k, wear something disposable. NO EYE CONTACT.'

Juliet blinked at the screen, utterly baffled. The message

was obviously intended for someone else but she was fascinated by the codes. What the hell did 'bdsm' mean? Suddenly the whole terrible break-up scene was forgotten as she tried to figure out what the cryptic text was about. Had she intercepted a message for a secret agent?

Then the penny dropped. Hotel plus money meant escort! While she'd been sitting here trying to force down her risotto Milanese as Matt laid out all the reasons why they weren't compatible after eight and a half months, some man – rich by the look of it – had been making requests to be forwarded to a call girl. Juliet wondered what the intended call girl was doing right now. Perhaps she was having a lovely expensive meal with a client. Would the person who had sent the text wonder when they didn't hear back from her?

Juliet glanced at the remains of her dinner, at her half-empty glass of Pinot Noir. Matt had thrown up his hands once she'd started crying and then he'd sent for the bill. He stayed long enough to give her the old chestnut that it was him, not her, and then he'd abandoned her to the stares of the other diners.

Now that she had recovered from the initial shock, she thought of all the things she should have said. It wasn't like she didn't have any complaints about *him*. He was far from perfect. Hadn't her friends been telling her as much for months? OK, so she could be a bit stubborn. A bit reckless. And yeah, she was a bit of a drama queen. But she could fill a book with *Matt's* flaws. He was a fool to think that the venue would have made a difference to how she reacted to being dumped. Still, she gave him credit for not doing it via text.

She felt a smile tugging at the corner of her lips as she glanced down at the phone again. What if … No. It was crazy. Hell, it was bloody dangerous! She shook her head as she picked up her handbag and coat. Despite the pitying smile he'd given her earlier, the waiter looked relieved that she was finally going. Her eyes fell on her watch as she buttoned her coat. It was 7.30.

Juliet wasn't considering anything reckless, definitely not. But perhaps she ought to reply to the text, just to let the sender (pimp? Madam?) know it had reached the wrong person. Yes. That would be the polite thing to do. She hit 'reply' and her fingers hovered over the keypad.

The Montefiore was the poshest hotel in the city. And a man who could afford to stay there *and* order out for sex *and* pay £1,000 for it couldn't possibly be a serial killer. Besides, would a psycho really leave a trail like this to be followed?

All day Juliet had been looking forward to this evening. A nice meal in her favourite restaurant followed by a night of rampant sex. Except Matt didn't really do 'rampant', did he? In fact, it often seemed like he was only going through the motions for her, ticking off an item on a to-do list so he could get back to his XBOX and blow shit up. Maybe he didn't even fancy her.

Maybe he'd actually done her a favour.

Before she knew what she was doing she had typed a message back. 'I'll be there,' it said. She hit 'send' and her stomach immediately began to flutter. She had just enough time to run home, clean up her face and get changed. *Wear something disposable.* No problem. She had plenty of things she wouldn't mind having ripped off her if this guy liked things a bit rough. *She* certainly did. As to whatever those codes meant ... Well, she'd find out, wouldn't she?

It didn't take her long to decide that the outfit she'd worn to Matt's birthday bash was disposable. She'd picked it out just for him because it was tight and red and showed off her ample cleavage. Well, now someone else was going to enjoy that ample cleavage and more besides. Better still, there was £1,000 in it for her.

She shoved her feet into the red stilettos that were half a size too small for her. One of those ridiculous impulse buys she'd succumbed to one day which now sat gathering dust in her wardrobe. She would be limping by the end of the night but so what? A thousand pounds would buy a lot of fancy shoes. Ones that actually fitted.

It had just gone eight when she arrived at the hotel, where she sat in the car trying to bolster her courage. She kept checking her phone in case someone had rumbled her but there were no new messages. Finally, she belted her coat and forced herself to go in. The lobby was a palatial marble affair that took her breath away. At first she wasn't sure where to go and she was terrified to ask at reception. Surely they would spot her. As the real thing or as a fake, it didn't matter. Either way she'd be in trouble.

Then she heard a man announce loudly to his wife that he was going to fetch something from his room and Juliet trailed after him, pretending she knew where her own room was. She rode up in the lift with him and felt faintly disappointed when he didn't even spare her a glance. He got off on the sixth floor and she continued on up.

She panicked before it reached nine, hitting the button for eight so she could get off and calm her jangling nerves. Maybe this was a mistake. She could still chicken out; she hadn't passed the point of no return. No one would ever know.

Looking up, she noticed her reflection in an elegant gold-framed mirror opposite the lift. A sexy young woman stood there, her coat not entirely concealing the charms on offer underneath. She had a great figure, that girl. Glossy blonde hair that cascaded over her shoulders. Glittering green eyes and full, pouty lips. She undid the belt of her coat for a proper look and nodded approval at the shapely body now on display. Curves in all the right places and legs that didn't stop.

'I'm doing it,' she told herself decisively.

She got back into the lift and this time she didn't hesitate when she reached the ninth floor. Room 903 was at the end of the hall and she realised with some dismay that she was late. Only about ten minutes but what if he'd given up and called for someone else?

As she raised her fist to knock it suddenly occurred to her to wonder about the man. She had considered and dismissed the possibility that he was dangerous but she hadn't given a single thought to what he might look like or how old he might be. What if he was hideous and ancient? Or looked like her father? Or Matt?

She was still standing there, wide-eyed and trembling with uncertainty when the door opened. For a moment she simply froze, forgetting why she was there. Then she gathered her wits and forced a smile for the man who was no older than forty and really quite striking.

'Hi,' she said. 'I'm sorry I'm late. I'm Juliet.'

The man – her *client*, she reminded herself – frowned. 'What do you think you're doing?' he asked softly.

Taken aback, Juliet didn't know what to say. She glanced behind her in case he was addressing someone else.

'Yes, I'm talking to you,' he said sharply. 'Were the instructions unclear?'

She gasped as she remembered. *No eye contact.* How could she have forgotten such a weird detail? Immediately, she lowered her head and fixed her gaze on his polished black shoes. *Slave*, she reminded herself. That was in there too.

'That's better. Let's start again, shall we? And this time I don't want you to speak.'

Before she could even nod he closed the door. She shuddered, feeling like an admonished schoolgirl. But something about his brusque manner had excited her. But something about his brusque manner and deep rumbling voice had excited her and she squirmed a little as she waited for him to open the door again.

When he did she was already looking down at the floor, her hands clasped demurely behind her back.

'Hmm,' he said, and she sensed him looking her over. 'Yes, you'll do. In you come.'

She obeyed and stepped into the most lavish hotel room she'd ever seen. Marble fireplace, four-poster bed, carved ceiling, the works. She had to remind herself not to gawk; she was an escort and presumably used to such luxury.

'Take off your coat.'

She jumped at the instruction and quickly did as she was told. He took it from her and dropped it over the back of a leather armchair. Then he stood to one side, regarding her.

'Yes, very nice,' he said at last. 'Now, since it seems no one has explained the rules to you, I advise you to pay attention. I am your master and that is how I expect to be addressed. With every word and every movement you will demonstrate your submission to me. You do not speak unless spoken to, nor will you look me in the eyes. You are a slave and you must learn your place.'

Juliet's face burned as he laid it out for her and she felt herself melting into the role, becoming meek and obedient even as he told her she must be. She had often entertained submissive fantasies, but it had never occurred to her that anyone else had similar ideas.

He seemed to be waiting for something and at last she whispered, 'Yes.' She hesitated a moment, then swallowed and said it. 'Master.' The word felt delicious on her tongue, like a fine wine that took time to reveal the full range of its flavour.

'Very good. Now go stand in front of the fireplace.'

She did as she was told, her heels clicking on the marble. Her feet were already throbbing and she tried to hide her immense relief as he told her to remove her shoes. She prised them off and set them neatly to one side, enjoying the chill of the marble beneath her burning soles.

The man turned away and went to fetch something from the bedside table. She heard the jingle of metal and began to tremble in anticipation of whatever he was going to do to her. The gusset of her panties was already very wet.

He returned and stood before her. He dropped a small cushion at her feet and said simply, 'Kneel.'

A hot blush suffused her with warmth and she sank to her knees as if in a trance, her heartbeat throbbing in her ears. He instructed her to gather her hair out of the way and she piled it on top of her head, holding it there while he fastened something cold and metal around her neck. Even without seeing it she knew what it was: a slave collar. The thought both frightened and excited her.

He withdrew a tiny lock from his pocket and she closed her eyes as he slipped it through the trailing links of the collar and clicked it shut. He told her to stand again and for a moment she wasn't sure she could manage it. Her legs felt incapable of supporting her. But already she found herself so powerfully eager to please him that the thought of failing such a simple task was unthinkable. She got slowly, if unsteadily, to her feet, keeping her eyes downcast. Her hands were still pinning her hair on top of her head but she didn't dare relax them. Not until she was told she could.

'You learn fast,' he said, sounding pleased. 'Stay just as you are.'

He placed his hands on either side of her and directed her forwards a little. Her body vibrated with the energy in his touch and she felt her pulse quicken. Then her breath caught in her throat as he took something down from the mantel behind her. A pair of scissors.

He held them in her line of sight for a few seconds and she knew immediately what he was going to do. He slipped the cold implement between her leg and the hem of the dress and she held her breath as he made the first cut. The blades purred against the fabric as they made their way up her thigh, severing the dress and exposing her a bit at a time. He stopped just short of her knickers and made another slit on the opposite side. He took his time, clearly savouring the slow reveal.

It was driving Juliet mad. She'd pictured a scene of wild passion with a brute who would pin her down and rip her clothes from her violently before fucking her senseless. It was an image she often masturbated to. Now she knew it was forever surpassed by this. She trembled as she stood, hands on her head, submitting to the careful, measured exposure.

He drew his hand over the swell of her chest and Juliet gave a little gasp at the touch. Then he slipped the scissors into the front of the dress and began snipping downwards. The dress sprang apart, instantly displaying the lacy red plunge bra that barely contained her breasts. Her nipples were hard little knots beneath the fabric.

He stopped at her navel and stood back to admire his handiwork. Juliet's arms were beginning to ache but she hoped he wouldn't tell her to lower them. It was a strangely erotic pain. It was something she was enduring to maintain the appealing posture for her master. The thought made her shudder with desire and for a moment she felt light-headed.

He returned and with two quick snips he cut the shoulder straps. The ruined dress fluttered to her feet like a shed skin. Now he stood regarding her again and Juliet held her breath as he slipped the scissors into the centre of her cleavage and severed her bra. The cups fell away, releasing her breasts and showing him her stiff pink nipples. Her panties were next. Looking down she could see the wet patch in the gusset as they succumbed to the blades and drifted to the floor with the rest of her clothes.

The man returned the scissors to the mantel and walked around her, inspecting her naked body as though she were a statue he were thinking of exhibiting. When she felt his touch at last she gasped, but she made herself hold still. He drew the backs of his fingers down one side of her ribcage, fitted his palm over a jutting pelvic bone, gently stroked the inside of one thigh. Each time he touched her he came tantalisingly close to the places she most wanted to feel his hands, but each time he denied her.

'Lovely,' he murmured at last, and Juliet arched her back, presenting herself. The position forced her chest up like an offering, one she was getting desperate for him to accept.

But he turned away again, removed his jacket and

arranged it neatly across the back of a chair. As he did, Juliet stole a peek at his face. His features were smooth, calm, utterly unruffled. He was a man in total control of his environment and everything in it. He would take his time with her. Her needs and wants were irrelevant here. She was here to please him. Quite beyond being her master in fantasy, he was her client for the night. Both roles spun together in her mind, making her dizzy with desire.

She heard the jingle of metal again and saw that he had another delicate length of chain in his hand. This one had little clips on each end and she blinked in confusion at them.

Without a word, he reached up and cupped her right breast in his hand. After so much teasing, the contact was electric. She closed her eyes with an ecstatic sigh as he lightly pinched the nipple between his thumb and forefinger, awakening every nerve in her body. Then the pressure intensified and she looked down to see he was fastening one of the clips to her nipple. He slowly eased the jaws closed, gauging her response. She gritted her teeth and hissed, a little frightened as the unfamiliar sensation grew from pleasure to something that was almost pain but not quite.

'Breathe,' he said.

She obeyed, drawing in a slow deep breath and relaxing into the pressure. He applied the other clip to her left nipple and she shuddered as she tried to stand still. Her arms were really getting quite sore now and her nipples burned with the intense pressure and relentless stimulation. And yet it was a strange sort of discomfort. The fact that it gave him pleasure was only a small part of it. There was a bizarre sense of achievement as well for enduring it. The helplessness, the exposure, the pleasure, the pain ... It all blurred together in her mind, creating a heady blend of sensations she could no longer process individually.

'Such a good girl,' her master said, his deep voice soothing and encouraging. 'I know it's difficult, but you do want to make me proud, don't you?'

Warmth flooded her body at his words and she lowered her head even further. 'Yes, Master.'

It was very hard to stand still with the constant pressure on her nipples. She was unable to keep from squirming a little. Nor could she stop herself squeezing her thighs together. Her sex pulsed in response, growing even wetter as she silently begged him to take her.

She had no idea how long she stood there, suffering and submitting, but when he approached her again to remove the clips she was almost disappointed.

He cradled her breast in his hand as he prepared to release the first clip and she knew without his telling her that it would hurt. Sure enough, he pinched the jaws apart and blood surged back into her tortured nipple, making

69

her cry out in pain. She held her breath as he released the other one and this time she only whimpered.

She could see his smile out of the corner of her eye and she knew she had pleased him. Her nipples throbbed with the returning sensation, making her crave his touch even more. She wanted his hands on her, his lips, his tongue. Most of all she wanted his cock. She could see the hardness in his trousers and she marvelled at his self-control.

When he took hold of her wrists and lowered her arms she had nearly forgotten they were up there. Sensation flooded into both limbs with an equally intense rush that made her gasp and he led her, shaky and unsteady, to the bed. He swept her into his arms and laid her on it. The softness beneath her was exquisite after the ordeal by the fireplace and she closed her eyes, melting into its velvety comfort.

She heard the zip of his trousers and listened to the quick flutter of his fingers as he undid the buttons of his shirt. Then she felt the warmth of his naked flesh as he mounted her and pushed his length into her wet, hungry sex and began to fuck her.

Juliet flung her arms out to the sides, clutching the bedclothes as she surrendered to pleasure of a kind she'd never known was possible. Her body was wildly alive, as though experiencing joy for the very first time.

She wrapped her legs around him and he lowered his

head to her breasts, kissing and licking her sensitive nipples into further arousal. He slid a hand between their bodies, stroking her clit even as he thrust deeper and deeper inside her. It was almost too much, almost more than she could take. In seconds she felt herself teetering on the edge and then she was over it, screaming as a powerful climax consumed her. His own merged with hers, intensifying it with the spasms of his cock inside her.

It seemed like hours before she could move again. She lay limp and spent, gazing across the room at the remnants of her clothes when suddenly, unexpectedly, her eyes filled with tears. She didn't want this to end. She didn't want to go. She didn't want to return to the boring, mundane world of men who asked tentatively if they were hurting her or otherwise just pounded away like farm machinery with no thought for her own pleasure. She didn't want to be thanked for a nice bit of sport, paid and sent out into the night again. But more than anything, she didn't want to have to take off the slave collar.

Her client didn't ask what was wrong and she only cried harder as the fantasy disintegrated in her mind's eye. Maybe if she were lucky he'd think she was worth the money and ask to see her again sometime, if she even got out of this without being reported to the police or hunted down by the escort whose assignment this was meant to be. And, oh God, she hadn't even thought about leaving afterwards! Her clothes were ruined and she hadn't thought to bring anything else to wear.

'I can guess what's going on in your mind,' he said at last with a trace of amusement, 'but things aren't what you think they are.'

She sniffled and wiped her eyes. 'What do you mean?'

He rolled her onto her side so she was facing him. Out of habit she lowered her gaze but he laughed softly and raised her head so she could meet his eyes at last. 'I saw you in the restaurant tonight. In fact, I've seen you there several times. I could tell what you wanted, what you needed. Because I could tell you were my perfect counterpart.'

Juliet shook her head in bewilderment. 'What are you talking about?'

'I sent that text.'

Completely lost, she could only stare at him.

'It's my restaurant, you see. And, luckily for me, you always book your table online and leave your mobile as a contact number.'

She blinked in disbelief at the elaborate scheme for several seconds before she could speak again. 'But – how did you know I'd respond to the text?'

He shrugged. 'If you hadn't you wouldn't have been the girl for me. But I know an adventurous girl when I see one. Especially one who secretly wants to be tamed.'

Juliet lay back on the bed, reeling. Her body was still

tingling from the escapade and now her mind was flooded with hope and the sense of possibility.

'But where are my manners?' he said, sitting up. 'You had an appalling time in my restaurant tonight and I would feel terrible if I didn't remedy it.'

'But my dress,' she protested. 'I can't go back out. I didn't bring anything else to wear.' Tears brimmed in her eyes again at her stupidity.

'Hush,' he said firmly. 'I'll have the chef send over some food and a bottle of wine. And also some lemon cheesecake. I notice you never have the tiramisu.'

She blushed at the revelation of how attentively he'd been watching her movements, at the total control he had over her. She squirmed as she imagined kneeling at his feet as he fed her dinner and dessert, one bite at a time, one sip of wine at a time. And she began to smile as she realised she wouldn't have to take the collar off at all.

No Strings
Primula Bond

The dress felt gorgeous, sea-green chiffon stroking and skimming my legs like breath, and you could tell by the way the skirt rippled that it was exquisitely cut.

'Totally different sensation when you're not wearing knickers, isn't it? The material tucks right into your fanny, if you'll let it. I must say you've a sensational figure. Perfect for business,' commented Joan, cocking her head to examine me. 'Can't think why we haven't seen you here before.'

My lips were too dry to answer. Joan's plump rouged face peered over my shoulder in the mirror, her yellow hair razored into submission. Her hard blue eyes glittered under so much eye shadow that it was impossible to read her expression.

She gathered my hair up into her fist and let it fall, swinging over my bare shoulders and down my back.

'For this occasion you are perfect. Tall, slim, auburn hair. Young. And you've surprisingly big tits, haven't you? They have to be real for this job. No fakes. Perfect the way they're practically falling out of that bodice, just the way they like it, yet you must give the impression of being pretty cool. Most of all, they like the girl to make like she's totally new to all this. A virgin in all but hymen. Get my drift?' Joan cleared forty years of smoking from her throat. 'A paradox. An ingénue, who looks like she's secretly oozing experience. That's what keeps them on their toes and wanting more. Let's hope you'll be worth every penny.'

I searched her painted features to learn her own history. She could have been anyone, or anything. She spoke like a gangster's moll, but equally she could have been a schoolteacher or a bus conductor. Her skill was in her disguise. But me? I was even more transparent than my dress. A naive creature barely out of her gymslip, who had lied about her age just to get through the door.

As Joan fiddled with the spaghetti straps of the dress, I wondered, with a churning in my stomach, what I had let myself in for.

'Now tonight they want you to go to the house for a garden party. It's unusual, but it's an advantage for you, as you're new to this, and it's also an honour for us. Normally it's hotels, or restaurants, or the theatre, or business functions. But if you're being entertained in someone's private property, you've got to be charming and decent, give absolutely nothing away except what they will coach you to say for the benefit of the people around them. And of course be ultra respectable.'

'No problem,' I croaked, stretching my lips into a smile and feeling the soothing slick of the pale lipgloss settling across them.

'I know it's no problem, dear.' Joan's voice hardened, and she pushed me away from her to cross to her desk. 'We don't "do" problems in this business. I know I've taken you on at the last minute but you look the part. Classy, well spoken, though don't speak too much, and hot. Be ready to turn on the charm so that everyone will envy the client. If anyone else tries it on with you, be discreet. You can't let on you're for hire, because that outs the client. But if all is revealed anyway by the end of the evening then, hey, you're reeling in fresh meat. You'll be bringing back plenty of cash, that's the main thing. Otherwise it's back to Milton Keynes or wherever it is you come from.'

Her disdain worked wonders. A knot of anger tightened in my chest, stamping out my anxiety. She picked up the telephone and waved me away. I would show her what I was made of. The anger changed shape, surged through me in a curling wave, and I was out on the pavement hailing a cab before she could say 'suspenders'.

The city was steaming in a heatwave, but the light was paling into evening. It's how I love London best. Joan didn't know it, but I came from just around the corner in Portobello Road. We all knew exactly what trade she plied behind the stained-glass door. Anyone spotting me would know exactly what I was up to. The danger made it all the more thrilling.

People were already settling themselves outside bars and cafés. I envied them, drinking and relaxing, and I even spotted a couple of my mates outside the Rising Sun pub, but they wouldn't have recognised me. Back then my usual attire was tattered jeans and biker vests, but that first night I may as well have been invisible, teetering past in my chiffon minidress and fuck-me heels, because I was about to enter a world far removed from my carefree existence.

My sweaty thighs stuck to the plastic seat of the taxi as it rumbled through the sluggish traffic, and my sex lips let out a damp kissing sound as I shifted about on my butt. I lifted one leg then the other off the seat and heard the moist sound again, and my pussy twitched with the wicked knowledge that there was nothing covering it, bare beneath my dress, nothing between the tight curls of my bush and an unknowing world. I caught the eye of the driver. What would he think if he knew I wasn't quite the posh young lady I seemed, going to a smart garden party in Knightsbridge? What would he think if he knew that these same sticky thighs would be spreading on a bed or a floor in a big white house any minute now, opening for some guy who had never seen me before and who might be passing me off as his wife or fiancée, or business associate, perhaps introducing me to his titled parents and friends before getting rid of them and starting to unhook my lovely dress ...

'You going in there or what?'

The engine was idling and we were outside a tall townhouse in a quiet street behind Harrods. The driver was yawning and holding his hand out for money, reaching behind him to flick on his yellow FOR HIRE sign.

A pink and white striped awning covered the garden path, leading visitors round the side of the house. I walked between heavy-scented honeysuckle bushes to the back. I pulled my shoulders back, thrust out my tits and stepped onto the velvet green lawn.

There was nobody there. Only a pale girl in a white dress playing the harp. I listened to the watery music for a moment, teetering on the edge of the grass, and glanced around.

'Clara?'

An elegant woman in a long black sheath dress, with black hair coiled into the nape of her neck like a flamenco dancer, came through the French windows with two flutes of champagne and handed one to me. I took it without thinking and pressed the cold glass to my cheek. Silver bangles jangled on her arm as she lifted hers and puckered her lips to sip.

'Yes,' I answered after an expectant pause. My real name is Lou. 'I'm a friend of … of …'

Joan's face rose before me, red with fury. I was already forgetting my lines.

'I know who you are. It's fine. I'm so pleased you could come. What a lovely dress. Clings to every luscious curve.'

Her full red lips parted in a friendly smile. I smiled back, flattered by her remark. She looked like a woman of taste. We stood in the garden and listened in silence to the music.

'So. Where's Mr … Where's Nat?' I asked. Tempting as it would be to linger with this exotic woman all evening, I had work to do.

'There's only you and me here at the moment,' the woman said, taking me by the arm and walking me slowly along the colourful flowerbeds edging the lawn. 'Come and enjoy the garden.'

'And the harpist,' I said. 'What a wonderful place for a party.'

The pale girl was gazing up at the pinkening sky. Her long white fingers played over the strings as if they, too, were made of water. The black-eyed woman sat down on an oriental daybed covered in silk cushions, which was placed in an archway of vivid pink clematis. Big candles burned in tall holders around the luxurious bed and filled the evening air with a heavy scent. From here the harp music was like waves in the distance.

'You look tense. Come and sit with me,' she murmured, patting the seat beside her. I hesitated, then sank down on the soft mattress, still searching the garden for the arrival of my client. The breeze went right up under my skirt, wafting against my naked pussy, and I parted my legs. The moving air was delicious after the uncomfortable heat in the taxi, and I let the dress ride up my thighs.

'That's better. Relax, darling,' the woman went on in a low voice. 'You've come to the right place. All we do here is enjoy ourselves and welcome anyone who wants to join us.'

I looked round again for the 'we' she was referring to, but actually I was quite content, if she was, to enjoy myself with her in this scented garden until Nat came along to demand my services.

'You're much younger than you pretend, aren't you?' the woman remarked. 'Certainly younger than the agency said. No more than nineteen, maybe twenty, I'd guess.'

'Is that a problem?' I stammered, too late remembering Joan's words.

'We all lie to get ahead. And you're just on the threshold. A gorgeous woman just budding, like these lilac blooms. I wonder, have you had much experience? Sexual, I mean?'

I blushed. Be cool. Be sophisticated. Mysterious.

'Like you wouldn't believe. Especially overseas. I find travelling frees the inhibitions, you know?'

I didn't want her telling Nat that I was green or that I wasn't up to it, but was that a bit too much boasting? I bit my lip. But she only smiled all the more. She was gentle, but not like a mother, I realised. Not like a sister, either.

'Sweetheart, this isn't an interview! Of course you know what to do, beautiful girl like you,' she soothed, tipping my chin. 'All the boys would be flocking like bees to a honeypot. But I meant other experiences. With girls, perhaps?'

'I can do whatever you want me to do.' I flushed again, but this time the heat was rising through my body. 'Is that what Nat is into? Watching girls together?'

She shrugged and flipped my hair over one shoulder and started to stroke my face. I liked the compliments, coming from someone so beautiful, and her fingers were so gentle as they played across my skin.

'So you've been touched like this.'

She pulled me a little closer, one hand on my face and the other brushing my back. The dress was very low cut and was so light that it took me a while to realise that she was stealthily unzipping my dress, stroking me the while, her fingers travelling down my spine. I shivered as she touched the spot above the cleft of my buttocks.

'Plenty of times.' I swallowed.

'Sensitive there?'

Her voice was right against my ear and I nodded. Her face was close and I could smell the berry scent of her lipstick. She turned me gently to face her, and it felt so different from the rough way Joan had twisted me. This woman was mesmerising. I felt powerless to move, as if she had cast a spell on me, and anyway I had no desire to move. Either the champagne had gone straight to my head, or her touches and scents were intoxicating me.

She bent forwards in the silence and slid her dark-red lips across mine and paused, perhaps waiting for me to push her away. I flinched, cursed myself inwardly for giving myself away, and opened my mouth. The wet tip of her tongue slid like a cat's inside my top lip and it was as if a match had been struck inside me. She circled her tongue slowly inside both my lips and they quivered in response, unable to close over her tongue but wanting to keep it there, wondering how to go on. She closed her mouth, rested it against mine, and drew away.

'So lovely to be kissed, isn't it?' she cooed, so softly that I just nodded again, letting her smooth my hair back.

She slid the straps down my arms so that the chiffon fell away and my breasts bounced out. They looked bigger and more swollen since I had got dressed. My nipples met the evening air and shrank into tight points, sending darts of desire through my breasts and down to my loins. She lowered her eyes slowly and they gleamed. My nipples tingled as she looked at them, burning red, wanting attention.

Instinctively, I pushed my shoulders back, thrusting my tits towards her and with another big red smile she teased me, fanning her fingers over each breast as if measuring them. My skin rose in goosebumps, willing her to touch them, then she took each smooth mound in her hands and cupped them, squeezing them together and flicking the hard nipples with her thumbs so that I wriggled with excitement on the cushions and forgot everything except her face and her hands.

'Is this what happens?' I whispered. 'You prepare me for later?'

Still she just smiled. As she kneaded my breasts, slowly and deliberately, she saw me wriggle again and nudged her own leg between mine. The black silk of her dress fell away and I saw that though the garment appeared demure it was actually slit to the hip, and her coffee-coloured skin was bare. Everything in me yearned to get closer to her and her clever hands. I touched her leg, smoothing my hand up and down under the silky material, and she pushed her knee further in between my legs so that it nudged right up against my pussy. Her eyes widened as she felt the damp curls against the bone of her knee. I inched myself forwards, stroking right up to the top of her leg, and found that, like me, she was naked under the black dress.

I paused, unsure where to go next. But her skin was so warm that my fingers travelled across the top of her thigh and into the divide of soft flesh nestling there without thinking. I hesitated. She couldn't suss out that I had never seen, let alone groped, another woman's cunt before, but I was a quick learner and there was no stopping me now. I gasped as I touched the hidden petals. Not only was she naked, but she was waxed bare, as well. Her sex lips were like velvet and, as I stroked them, her leg twitched and her hands gripped my tits harder. Unable to contain my curiosity, I got up on my knees, crawled closer to her, and straddled her, settling myself on her lap.

I moaned quietly as I spread my legs over her crotch, grinding my pussy against hers. I tugged at her dress so that it came up round her waist. It was already spotted with damp patches. The neat curls of my bush brushed up against the tender skin of her labia and she gasped. A shiver of triumph went through me.

'My little pussy cat!' she murmured.

I wrapped my arms around her neck and bent down to lick at her soft cheeks and her big generous mouth.

'What was that you were saying about other

experiences?' I whispered against her lips. 'Show me what you want.'

Her tongue went right inside my mouth then, and, unlike kissing a man, she tasted of lipstick and champagne. Her tongue explored my teeth and tongue like a slippery cock and I sucked on it, trapping it before it escaped and swirled round again. I was breathing heavily now and I knew she could hear it, yet she was almost silent. I savoured her warm saliva and licked round her mouth as if she were a bowl of cream, daring her to stop me messing her lipstick, but she only responded more fiercely, bringing one hand up to tangle in my hair so that she could kiss me harder.

The harp music was slowing, and quieter. No one else had come into the garden.

Thank God, because my body was heating up and desire was building. I pulled away and knelt up a little so that I could push my breasts against her face. The woman looked up at me, her eyes burning, and, still holding my gaze, she extended her tongue from her still open mouth and flicked it at one of my nipples. Somewhere in the back of my mind I wondered if I should be doing that to *her*, but I was past the point of no return.

Her touch was electric and instantly my nipple shrank again into a rigid point. It tingled with expectation, and I angled my breast harder into her mouth, watching as she bared her teeth and nipped at it. Sheer fire crackled directly into my cunt as the sharp pain transformed into intense pleasure and she pinched the other nipple roughly with her fingers, biting and sucking each taut nipple in turn until I nudged my groin more urgently against her and she let herself fall backwards, pulling me down on top of her.

She continued to suck my tits, her big red mouth wet and sexy, as I crouched on all fours above her, and I felt for her pussy again and started to circle inside it with my fingers, bearing my weight with the other hand. Suddenly, I felt something tugging at my own butt, fingers pulling my butt cheeks apart, walking over the soft flesh, digging in, exploring, and for a moment I thought it must be my dark-haired lover.

But she was underneath me, still biting my nipples and the puckered skin around them, and both her hands were squeezing them like rising dough. I glanced over my shoulder and saw that the pale harpist had approached our garden boudoir and was standing behind me. The setting sun set her golden hair on fire but her blue eyes were still dreamy as she looked at my bare behind, my dress still clinging to my waist, then at my breasts hanging down over the other woman's face.

'May I?' she murmured, looking past me at the dark lady. Surely she should be asking *me*? The dark lady nodded.

'Of course, Flora. That's what you're here for. We can all do as we please.'

Something in her voice had hardened a little, and I looked back at her. Her black eyes glittered at me before she pulled my head down towards hers and kissed me again. The harpist's long fingers spread over my cheeks, holding them apart, and then her thumbs entered the crevice between and trailed up and down the shadowy skin, travelling down to the smooth bridge between my anus and my cunt, then back again.

The dark woman pulled herself back on her elbows from under me so that my tits brushed not against her lips but over her own full breasts. She paused as our breasts squashed against each other, and I started to sway from side to side, enjoying the sensation of soft flesh bouncing on soft flesh. As I swayed, the girl behind me grabbed harder onto my buttocks and pulled my legs further apart. One finger jabbed into my anus and I felt the little hole shrinking into itself. I recoiled, thinking she would stop, but she pushed her finger further in, the finger that a few moments earlier had been teasing such beautiful music out of her harp. As it pushed further up the tight tunnel, I felt the unfamiliar dirty pressure inside me filling that secret passage with a peculiar warmth, and my head started spinning.

I scrabbled with my free hand at my dark mistress's silk dress, which was loosely buttoned, and it fell away easily. I scooped out one brown breast and stared at it. Behind me, Flora paused, her musical fingers resting on my buttocks, one long finger still jabbed into my arse, and I wondered if she, too, was trying not to gasp out loud at the sight of the woman's beautiful breast swelling there, darker brown than her legs and with a tempting dark-red nipple standing out like a cherry.

The woman stopped smiling. She shifted herself more comfortably beneath me, flung her arms up behind her head and lay back amongst the cushions.

'Pleasure me,' she instructed, and lifted her hips towards my face. 'I am your mistress.'

I hesitated, looking at the narrow strip of black hair, the swelling brown sex lips glistening with moisture. What if Nat came out and found that I'd already started working on his hostess? She opened her legs for me, arched her back again so that her hips were higher, licked one finger and brought it down to circle her nipple.

I bent down, just as Flora the harpist started stroking my buttocks again. I ran my tongue up my hostess's wet crack and could hear the slurping of saliva on pussy juice. Her cunt smelled scented. She must have had a good douche before dressing, but there was still the strong sharp tang of female excitement. I licked again, slowly at first then faster as her body responded. She made no sound now, so I had to take my cue from the way her pussy pushed at me when I licked and shivered when I stopped.

Behind me, my harpist jabbed her finger harder up my arse again, and I could feel the cool touch of her skin on my bare back as she started to rub herself against me. I closed my eyes and parted the dark woman's pussy lips with my fingers, more roughly now, and sucked on the bright red clit that popped out from its hiding place, and then the dark lady couldn't help herself, she bucked wildly and let out a small moan, so I sucked even harder, and behind me the harpist thrust her finger in and out of my arse. I reached behind me to try to grab at her, found her free hand, and pushed it down towards my pussy, into my pussy, so she could play me like she played her harp, she could fuck me both ways. I was getting euphoric now with what was happening to us all, vaguely thinking it wasn't right that Flora wasn't getting any pleasure, perhaps it would be her turn next, and then I was coming, and so was the dark lady, her cunt squeezing shut around my fingers, my cunt in turn squeezing on Flora's fingers, and our moans only just drowned out by the traffic passing by on the other side of the wall.

The dark woman pushed me away and pulled her silk dress closed.

Flora came and sat on the bench beside her, and I stood awkwardly, my knees still knocking, tugging at my short dress. There was a long silence filled only by a couple of greedy bees diving into the apricot honeysuckle.

'I'm told not to ask, but as we're now so closely acquainted, what's your name?'

The pale harpist put her hand over her mouth in embarrassment, but it was too late. I'd overstepped some kind of mark. The dark lady jumped up and motioned for us both to follow her back round to the front of the house. The harp was in its case, waiting on the pavement, and a cab was idling there.

How had the harp been removed without us noticing?

'We're not closely acquainted, Clara. You're my paid tart. So that's for you,' my mistress said calmly, handing me a cheque.

She pressed a wad of cash into Flora's outstretched hand. 'And that's for you.'

We stood dumbly on the pavement. I was aware of Flora's slim white arm brushing against mine.

But as she turned to go back into the garden she said, 'OK, my name is Natalie. Nat for short!'

Don't I
Charlotte Stein

I don't know what I expect when I first step into the room. A mean-eyed creature, I suppose, with too much hair on his face and hands like shovels. He'll stand straight away and use said shovels to knock me around the room for a bit, most likely, though I'm not sure where that assumption comes from.

Movies, I think. Movies, in which the heroine is always punished for doing something as desperate as selling her body for cash. Of course, in these movies the hero usually swoops in and saves her right before she's gang-raped or worse, but somehow I suspect that isn't going to happen here.

It's just this. It's just me, in a dress made for a smaller woman and heels too high for my body to cope with, red lipstick shining incongruously on my plain as paper face. And when he looks at me – this client – I feel all of these things even more keenly than I thought I would.

Because he isn't hairy at all. He doesn't have shovel hands, or an air of some underworld I don't understand. Instead, he's soft-mouthed and blue-eyed. Big, true, but not in the way I'd expected. I'd thought of grizzly men who've earned the term 'brick shithouse', but instead there's just this odd fullness to him. As though he lives just ever so slightly on the edge of delicious excess.

Too many cakes, I think, but that's unfair – and not entirely true. It doesn't look like he's eaten too many cakes at all. It looks as though he's been filled with something else altogether, and just when I think my mind can't get any stranger it writes in the correct description for me.

It's like he's been filled with come.

Of course I flush red the second I've thought it. Not because it's too rude, but because I know it's rude and yet it seems to perfectly fit him, anyway.

That's what he looks like. Like someone who's just had his ass fucked by ten men, and is now absolutely swimming in jism. It's running down his thighs, inside those immaculately tailored trousers he's wearing. He can still taste it at the back of his throat, when he swallows.

And somehow this thought is more paralysing than

the other one, about the brutal men who want to gang-rape me. For a long moment I just stand in the middle of the room, while this obviously refined and certainly handsome gentleman looks at me without a single idea of what I'm thinking in his head.

He's probably the son of an oil magnate. He's probably Christian Vanderhoof the Third. Really he has absolutely no clue what he's doing here, and very soon he's going to tell me to turn down the bed and clean the bathroom.

Only then he says: 'Would you care for a drink?'

And after that I don't know what to think. His voice is extremely cultured, his tone utterly polite. Everything about him is coated in a protective sheen of fabulous wealth, and yet I'm certain I can hear something underneath it all. A little burr of nervousness, I think, that doesn't quite fit my preconceptions of this evening.

Why is *he* nervous? He paid a thousand pounds for me. I can't even sneeze without his permission – though to look at him you wouldn't think it. He shifts in his chair, awkwardly, in a way that suggests he's impatient for my answer.

He's impatient, but he won't demand it.

'I'm fine,' I tell him, though in truth I'd love a Scotch. I can see from the empty glasses on the table next to him that he's had three, though I can't see why he needed a fresh container each time. Or why he needed so many.

Clean Dutch courage, I think, then feel a strange little surge go through me. *Yes*, that surge says. *He likes things clean and neat and ordered. He likes things a certain way – a new glass for each drink. Each one exactly the same, with a curl of lime and two ice cubes.*

And he needs the alcohol to steady his nerves, because he's never done this before.

'I suppose … you just want to get started.'

Oh, *definitely* never done this before. It's like looking in a mirror, for a second, though I suspect my half of the reflection is starting to seem a little different. I *feel* a little different, though I'm not sure why.

Because of the row of glasses? Because of the look of him and the way he stands, hands still flat on his thighs? All of the above, I think, and then I simply watch as he starts peeling off his clothes.

I won't deny it: it's almost a treat. I've never even dated a man half as handsome as this, and here he is, paying me for the privilege. And it *is* a privilege. His shoulders are broad, his chest big and solid. When he moves, things flex and shift beneath the skin.

And that's before I even get to his thighs – dear God, his thighs. They're thick and solid and curved in places I've never seen a man's thighs curve, though after a moment I have to look away from them. I have to.

He's hard. And though I know that's what I'm here for, and understand the rules of this game utterly, it's still something else to see it in the flesh. To have to face it, and know that's what my purpose is.

Even if I can feel my purpose shifting, as we speak. It's like it's poised on the top of a sand dune, and the more time ticks by the further down it slides, until I'm suddenly at the bottom, in a heap. I'm looking and looking at his thick, stiff cock, and I'm not exactly afraid, any more.

I'm not exactly anything. I'm just staring like I've stepped outside myself, and when he says: 'Do you know what I want you to do?' I don't tell him what I should. I don't say, *No, not really*. I just stand there and examine every naked inch of him, with this strange lewd sort of detachment.

And he seems to see it that way, too. In fact, after a long, long moment of staring, he actually says as much. He shivers once, all over, before telling me how good it feels to be looked at like that. Then once he's managed to force those words out, he goes one step further.

'Like a possession,' he says, but I swear I have no idea what he means. Is he suggesting that I should stand there, naked, while he maps *me* out with his gaze? It certainly seems as though it needs to be that way around, but here's the thing – I'm not sure it is.

He told me that *he* feels like the possession. That *my* eyes are the cruel, cold ones, judging the various parts of him. And when I really think about it, I *am* judging him. I judged him before I even walked into this room, and doing so now just feels like a natural extension of that. It's like armour – I need it.

I just didn't think he'd want it. I thought he'd have a little tool, rusted and mean. And the second I stepped in here he'd get that tool beneath the metal plating covering my skin, and lever it all off.

But he doesn't.

Instead, he says, 'What do you want me to do now?'

While inside I rise and fall, all at the same time. I get to choose – is that what he's saying? That I get to choose what happens now? I can hardly believe it, but before I've even worked up the courage to actually ask him he says it again. And this time, he says it far more clearly.

'Tell me what to do,' he says, the safety of that question mark now long gone. He looks like he doesn't want the safety of a question mark any more, anyway – as though little extra things like those ones have held him back.

But of course he doesn't have to hold back, with me.

And for the first time I realise something strange, something that hadn't even occurred to me before this moment. How could it possibly? This is a horrible thing, a painful experience I've been forced to endure. There is nothing pleasant about selling your body, I'm certain of it.

Or at least I'm certain until I think of those words,

when applied to me: *I don't have to hold back with him.* He isn't my boyfriend, who's likely to dump me if I do something forbidden in bed. He's not a one-night stand that might spread the urban legend of the girl who likes to lick a guy's asshole.

He's my client. And now he's said: *Go ahead.*

'Get down on all fours,' I say – just to test it out, I suppose. He can always laugh and say no at this point if he likes. There's still a chance I've gotten the wrong end of the stick, after all, and I wouldn't hold it against him.

Only then he does exactly as I've told him. He does it. This big, smooth-as-silk-looking guy gets down on his hands and knees on this expensive carpet and, as he does so, his eyes flutter closed. As though the whole thing is just too much to take, before we've barely done anything at all.

I understand how he feels, however. My legs seem weaker than they did when I first walked in here, and somewhere inside me there's this new sensation, blooming – one that gets stronger when I tell him to crawl towards me.

And he does.

'You like it down there?' I ask, though I don't really feel like I need to. It's obvious he likes it down there. His cock is still hard and, even if it wasn't, there are other things that point the way. Things that shouldn't seem familiar to me – *Miss Vanilla* – but somehow are anyway.

Like the way he shudders when I walk around him. Like the way his head drops between his shoulders the second I toe the ripe curve of his perfect ass with the point of one shoe.

Of course, I realise then the appeal of footwear like this. They had seemed skyscraper high and uncomfortable before – a nuisance, more than anything. But now they're weapons. My shoe is a tool, like the one I imagined him having. And all I have to do is shove said tool between the cheeks of his ass, to get his armour off.

'*No*,' he says, but something unexpected happens when he does. I don't automatically think of what I should – that it's time to be nervous, now, and back off before he tells on me. Before there are consequences.

Instead, I imagine just how far I could go.

From here, it looks like a million miles spread out before me.

'No?' I ask, and there's something new in my voice, now. I'd call it *resentment*, but it isn't exactly. It's crisp and cold and almost mocking, instead – and he seems to know it.

That shuddering gets worse. One of his hands jerks beneath him, like a reflex, but I can't allow that any more than I could allow him to tell me *no*. Who does he think he is, telling *me* no?

Doesn't he realise I'm a professional?

'Get your hand away from your cock, boy,' I say, and then it's my turn to shudder. Because, of course, I'm *not* a professional. I'm not anything. I don't even know what this thing is that seems to be growing inside me.

I only know that it made me say 'boy' and it made me say 'cock', and both things pound hard on that door inside me. The one that's closed, currently, but clearly labelled: *You like this. You like this you like this it's making you wet.*

I swear, it isn't. I can't feel it, sliding slick and slippery between the lips of my cunt, as I circle him. I can't feel it soaking into the expensive panties I was given to wear, until they're near ruined.

I'm insensible, a professional, I'm stone.

Even when he plants one shaking hand back on the carpet, I'm stone.

'Touch it again and it won't just be the toe of my shoe you'll feel,' I say, though I have to admit – I don't know what it is he *will* feel. The stiletto heel? My fingers? The cock I don't have?

All three seem crazy, but then so is this. It's crazy, that he seems so shaken up, by so little. There's actual sweat gleaming on his broad back now, and all I have to do to make him shiver and moan is just hint at touching him. Just ghost my heel over his side until he squirms and actually begs.

'Please,' he says, in a tone I never thought someone like him could get to. 'Please.'

But for what? What's he pleading for me to do? I can't imagine it's just a straightforward fuck, now – though the thought flashes in me far brighter than it had before. I mean, it's possible that he'd let me pin him down, while I did it. It's likely he wants me to tie him to something, while I use his cock for my own greedy pleasure.

And if those are just my own desires coming to me, unbidden, well … is that really a problem? He doesn't seem to think it's a problem when I put my foot on his back, and dig that heel in until he lies flat to the carpet.

Quite the contrary. He seems to think it's the best thing anyone could ever do to someone else, and I know this because he tells me so. He moans and babbles incoherently, until real words finally manage to spill out of him.

'Oh, that's perfection,' he says, though I'm not sure how it can be. Doesn't it hurt to be abused like this? Isn't he dying inside to feel someone doing this to him? And if he is, why don't I care?

I should care, I think, as I reach down to grab a fistful of his hair. I should be better, I think, as I wrench his head up – one foot still in the small of his back, like someone starting a heavy piece of machinery. Bracing themselves to get every ounce of strength into it that they can.

'Is this perfection, boy?' I ask, and he tells me yes. He tells me to do a million things I shouldn't want to, things that involve the throat I've just bared to a knife I don't have, and when I do them ... God. God.

When I close my hands around his neck and choke him, just a little ... I don't know what that feeling is. I can't name it. It's like he's got that rusty thing beneath my armour anyway, without me knowing it, and suddenly I'm bare and bleeding.

'Take it,' I tell him as I press my face into his sweet-smelling hair, one hand on him, squeezing and squeezing. I could kill him, now, I think, but that's not the worst thing about all of this. No – the worst thing is the thought that comes afterwards.

He'd let me.

I pull away then. I have to. All of this is far, far too much, in the opposite way I expected it to be. I thought I'd be crying, by now, and I suppose I am, but they're not tears of pain. They're something else instead.

'Get up,' I tell him, once my back is turned to him. If I look when he stands, I'll lose control of myself. *I'll* be the guy with the shovel hands, wanting to take this as far as he's willing to go.

Though I suppose that's the kicker, isn't it? He's *willing*.

'Lie down on the bed, face up,' I say, gentler now. Softer, though certainly more breathless. In truth, it kind of feels as though oxygen has made a fist halfway up my chest and every time I try to suck more in it just cycles back. It just gives me a quarter of what I really need.

And that feeling gets worse when I allow myself to look at the shape he's made on the bed. All of his limbs so heavy, sprawled out for my delectation. Wrists crossed one over the other, above his head – like a vague idea he'd once had, of what submission should look like.

But that's OK, though. That's OK. I see the same formless pattern in my head the moment I close my eyes. I think I've been seeing it all my life and just hadn't known it. I hadn't listened.

I'm listening now.

'What are you going to do to me?' he asks, and it's like a song. It's like a song inside me, playing just loud enough for me to hear.

'I'm going to fuck you until you beg me for mercy,' I say, as I climb onto the bed. 'And if you come before I say you can, I don't know what I might do. Is that what you want, boy?'

Before, it was hard to meet his eyes. But it isn't any more. I just lean right down and meet that foggy blue gaze directly, one hand cupping his chin – like I've pincered him, I think, like he's mine – and murmur words against his lips.

'Do you want me to not know?'

His breath catches in his chest – I hear it. I almost feel it in the subtle shift of his body beneath mine. And then it comes right out of him, in that one perfect word I've so longed to hear. The one no one's ever said to me; the one that makes me lean down and offer him something I swore I wouldn't willingly.

'Yes,' he says, and I kiss him. I kiss him I kiss him I kiss him, through the dozens more he then gives to me. 'Yes, yes,' he says, as though it's the easiest thing in the world to just give in to someone.

To let them do whatever they want.

I want to tell him that it isn't, but then again I'm the one putting the condom on him. I'm the one shoving my dress up around my waist, as frantic and flustered as I've ever felt myself. For a long embarrassing moment I can't seem to get my panties off, and I just tangle over him, legs everywhere.

But then it's done and I'm naked there and he can see me, those eyes of his still full of the same thing they were before. Not *God you're clumsy* but *God, just take me, just fuck me*, and when I do he says the name I haven't told him.

He pants it, into my open mouth – hands still linked above his head. Everything about him just so ready to be used, in a way that makes me wetter, hotter, more desperate for it. I can feel the evidence of my arousal coating more than the lips of my sex, now, and every time I move, every time I slide against him, my clit swells. Pleasure swells with it, sweet and thick.

Though worse than all of this is how quickly he becomes sensible of it. He knows, the second I ease myself down on his solid cock – because of course he can feel it. He can hear it, all slick and filthy.

And though I can too, I think I hide my shame well. More than well, in fact. My voice still comes out as cool as a winter river, when I tell him what I want him to do.

'Lie still,' I say, though the moment I do that feeling courses through me. My clit becomes one long pulse between my legs, and more of my wetness coats him – because he's just a doll, now. He's a thing I'm using for my own pleasure, and he doesn't even seem to mind.

In fact, he does more than *not mind*. He gives me his utter obedience, through the tensing of the muscles in his shoulders. In the way his lips disappear into his mouth, as he struggles to hold himself motionless.

It must be an almost impossible task, I know. How could it not be? He's so aroused there's a flush spreading over his chest, and everything I do makes those little shudders pass through him, minutely.

And if I'm really honest, this thing we're doing – this slow up and down I've got going, on the thick length of his glorious cock – it's almost too much for me. It's almost making me ache somewhere low down in my belly, so God only knows how it must feel for him.

He wanted this. He paid for it. And now he's just got to lie there and take it, as a hint of some kind of impossible orgasm just rubs ever so lightly over my clit.

'Oh that's good,' he bursts out, after a moment of this agonising slide around the swollen head of his cock. I won't deny – it feels best there, right up against the front wall of my clenching cunt.

But I will deny that I want to say the same thing back to him. Instead, I do something very mean and very delicious, like maybe just grabbing a hold of his face again. And when he tells me, 'Yes, yes, do it,' I go one step further. There's always one step further with this man whose name I don't even know.

Like slapping, for example. I hadn't even thought about slapping, but the moment I do it – hard and sharp across his perfect face – he forgets he isn't supposed to be moving. He bucks up, jerkily, into the absolute mess of my slippery pussy, and I can't help it either.

I actually let out a sound, as his cock jams firmly against that little bundle of nerves inside me. And then again, as he seems to become sensible of what he's done, and lets his hips ease back down to the mattress.

Of course when he does so, his cock eases back down with it. Though I'm beyond admitting that this isn't incredible, now. I'm beyond anything, and that includes my own control it seems. My own control says, *Be calm, don't fuck him like this, don't slap him harder*, while my body squirms against that good, good feeling, and my hand lashes out to crack across his face.

'You like that, huh?' I ask, but it's almost like I'm saying it to myself. And the second I realise this, I answer in my own head: *Yes. Yes, I like your cock in me. I like seeing my handprint on your beautiful face, and I like knowing what it does to you.*

It makes him buck – that's what it does. It makes him stop holding his hands above his head and start gripping my hips, so that he can grind me down harder every time my slaps connect.

And God, they're really connecting now. They're directly related to the pleasure building in me, it seems, and the closer I get to that unbearable edge, the more viciously I do it – though he doesn't seem to mind. He's getting close too, I think – closer than he'd probably like to be – and there's something about this thought that gets me going, too.

Just the idea of him, holding off the bliss that's coming. Just the idea that he's struggling and straining with it, cock swelling inside me anyway, unbidden. All of the breath in his body caught somewhere inside his chest – the way it was for me, only moments ago.

Then finally his words, God, his words.

'Ohhh fuck I'm close – please. Please, let me do it. Please.'

But I can't. I can't – not yet. I'm too cruel, I'm too

full of feeling, I'm too not myself. I want to come first and, Lord, I know I'm going to. I can't even hold it off now, never mind denying it, and, when it finally breaks, I don't care about telling him so.

'I'm coming, oh, my God, I'm coming,' I say, because it's true. But also because of the look it produces, all over his face. He seems almost in awe, for a second – as though he's never seen a woman actually do it before, in the middle of weird encounters like this – and not even that thought can put me off.

The pleasure coils tight in my belly and then unravels all at once, forcing me to tighten hard around his still working cock. Making me shiver and moan in the exact way he's done for me all the way through this.

I understand now, I think. I get it. And if he still seems shocked that I do, well, that's OK. I can probably pretend that I didn't, once this is all over – and it *is* nearly all over. He's asking me over and over: 'Can I? Can I?' And though there's some remnant of that cruelty in me, I don't want to say no any more.

'Do it,' I tell him, and then I watch with my own kind of awe as he does. His back arches, his mouth opens. Near soundless cries of pleasure come out of him as his cock surges inside me.

It's almost a disappointment when it's over.

Almost.

Because you know – this isn't my real life. This is just

something I had to do, to pay a mortgage I'm too behind on. To save myself from worse, like maybe sleeping on the streets. It's not really something I enjoy, once it's done and I'm picking up my underwear and telling him yeah, sure, I'll be available again.

I won't be available again. I won't be – not even after I've looked into his hopeful face and seen him smile for me, almost shyly. Because the truth is I have my thousand pounds now, and I never have to do this again. I never have to climb those stairs, and feel all of these strange, mixed feelings, and look into this man's eyes while that surge of power goes through me.

I mean, after all, I do find all of this awful and abhorrent. I do, I really do.

Don't I?

Substitute
Aishling Morgan

The moment I heard the door bang I knew Tina was in a panic. I'd been trying to write my weekly essay, but I knew it was hopeless. Whatever had happened, she'd want to talk to me about it, and there would be no peace until I'd soothed her feelings. Sure enough, her voice floated up from the hall.

'Sarah, I need your help!'

I closed the book I'd been reading and saved my work. Gauge bosons were going to have to wait. 'Just coming.'

Nobody else was in, and I knew the routine. She'd stay down in the kitchen, full of news of some dramatic event, good or bad. When it was good she'd be full of energy and excitement, eager to tell me all about what had happened. When it was bad she'd huddle into herself and need to be coaxed into talking to me. Either way, I'd get out the biscuits and make the tea. This time, to my surprise, she came upstairs, all the way to my room, appearing in the doorway like some careworn elf, all windswept blonde hair and skinny limbs.

'I need your help, Sarah! I'm double-booked this evening and there is no way I can do both gigs, just no way. You're going to have to do one for me. Mr Ridley he's called. He's a plant manager out at Cowley and –'

'Tina, slow down! What do you mean you're double-booked? I can't do your work, not your evening work.'

'Why not? Don't be difficult, Sarah, I need you!'

'But you work as an escort! I can't –'

'Don't be silly, of course you can. You're cute, or you would be if you put some make-up on and did your hair and made a bit of effort with your clothes. Come on, Sarah!'

'Yes, but Tina –'

I wanted to tell her I wasn't a tart, but I knew how hurt she'd be, and that my objection made no moral sense. She didn't let me finish anyway.

'Sarah! Don't be difficult. Look, it's just this once, and you can keep half the money. He's Mr Ridley, and you're to meet him at the Anchor –'

'Tina, please, I didn't say I'd do it. Look, I ... I can't handle what you do. I just don't have your way with people, and I'm not nearly attractive enough.'

'Of course you are, silly. When I've finished with you,

110

he'll think he's died and gone to heaven. He wanted a redhead anyway, so you're perfect, and he's a very polite old gentleman. He always brings flowers, and –'

'Old? How old exactly?'

'Forty, maybe forty-five. Well, he can't be much over fifty, or he'd have retired, but the old ones are easier, much more polite and considerate. And with Mr Ridley you get to go on top, or maybe doggie –'

'Tina! I haven't said I'd do it. I can't just fuck random guys.'

'Oh come on, Sarah, you've been out on dates and ended up in the sack before now, haven't you? What about that guy the week before last, Dan or Don, or whatever he was called, the nerd with the rucksack.'

'You mean Evan. He was my date, and he's brilliant. He got a First.'

'He looks like an upside-down mop with a couple of cabbage leaves glued to the sides, and he dresses like he robbed a charity store. Mr Ridley's smart, always in a suit and tie, and he's experienced, and he has a nice cock. It's not true, what they say about fat men –'

'So he's fat too? How fat?'

'So you'll do it?'

'I didn't say that.'

'You implied it, if you're worried about how fat he is. Come on, Sarah, I need you to do this for me, just the once. OK, you can keep all the money, how's that?'

'I am not going to bed with some fat old bastard from the plant.'

'Sarah! Why do you have to be so difficult? How can you do this to me? You're my best friend. He's not that fat, anyway, maybe fifteen, sixteen stone.'

'And how tall is he?'

'A bit taller than me. The same height, maybe.'

'Five three? And he weighs sixteen stone? He must look like a beach ball!'

'OK, OK, if you're going to be fussy, I'll do Mr Ridley and you can have Kojo Anan.'

'Who's he?'

'Kojo Anan, the footballer. He plays for Town. Don't you know anything? That's why it's better for you to have Mr Ridley, because with Kojo he'll expect you to know who he is, and he likes you to dress up in Town kit, so it's not really your thing at all.'

'And fat old businessmen are? So what's this Kojo like?'

'He's from Ghana, about six foot, kind of good-looking, but ... Really, Sarah, Mr Ridley would be much more your type.'

'No, he wouldn't.'

'OK, if you're sure you can handle him, you can have Kojo.'

'I haven't said I'd have anybody.'

'Oh shut up, Sarah. It's the deal of a lifetime, five

hundred quid to go with a guy like Kojo. Most girls would pay for him.'

'Why does he need an escort then?'

'He prefers it that way. He knows an escort will do as she's told, and he does like it quite rough, and then, not every girl will dress up for him. Mr Ridley –'

'I'm not going with Mr Ridley. I might go with this Kojo guy, but it's like you explained the other day, isn't it, he's just paying for my time? I don't have to have sex?'

'Not have to, have to, no, but he's going to expect it. Come on, Sarah, it's just one more willy, and I know you'll like it, 'cause I've heard you in bed with Evan, and Dr Whatsit, the one who's always perving over girls in jeans, and –'

'OK, OK, I'll go, but I'm doing you a huge favour here, Tina, and you're not to tell anybody else, anybody at all.'

She'd been bouncing from place to place around the room as we spoke, and came to kiss me before taking one more bounce back towards the door.

'Thank you, thank you, thank you. Oh, and for goodness sake don't tell him you're a Physics student. He'll think you're a geek. In fact, don't tell him you're a student at all.'

She was about to disappear back down the stairs, and I called out quickly, 'Hang on, Tina, don't go. Where am I supposed to meet him? And you said you'd help me get ready.'

Her voice came back to me from halfway down the stairs. 'At the club bar, stupid, and don't worry, it's OK to look scruffy in football kit.'

* * *

I certainly looked scruffy, but that wasn't what was making every single person walking past the Town football ground stare at me. Tina had explained that I needed to be in football kit, but not that it could only be purchased at the club shop. That had meant going straight there, with no time to get back home to change, so I'd been forced to make my purchases then and there, and get into them in the changing room. Nor had she told me that the club didn't cater for women, so that the only top that came close to fitting me across my shoulders also left every contour of my breasts showing as if it had been painted on my skin, while my shorts were so baggy around my waist it felt as if they would fall down at any second, but indecently taut across my bottom. Then there were the club colours, black and yellow hoops. They were nicknamed the Bumblebees, and I looked like one, or at least the cartoon caricature of one as drawn by an oversexed and distinctly kinky teenage boy. It was no surprise that people were staring.

My only consolation was that once I was safely in the club bar I wouldn't be the only one dressed like a clown, or so I thought. The doorman paused only long enough to let his eyes travel down from my hastily improvised and very shaggy red ponytail to my yellow and black football boots before treating me to a knowing wink and letting me past. Inside, everything was black leather and chromed steel, while the only things I matched were the posters on the walls. Everybody, but everybody, was in a suit or smart casual dress, all very refined and expensive.

I stopped just inside the door, blushing, not sure what to do or what to say, until one of the men at the bar detached himself from his friends. He was tall, beautifully muscled and very, very black, also smiling and with a hand extended in welcome, which left me weak-kneed with relief. When he spoke his accent was pure BBC English, and he immediately pulled a chair up for me and ordered a bottle of champagne. I'd had no idea what to expect, maybe some flash guy who'd call me a bitch and expect me to wiggle my bottom for him before he took me roughly from behind, and it was all too easy to give in to his easy charm. After a couple of glasses of champagne I was beginning to wonder why Tina always claimed to work so hard for her money, and by the time we'd got on to the second bottle I was laughing and joking with him and several of his friends, all young, athletic men who looked as if they'd be able to handle me very well indeed. It was almost a shame when Kojo stood up and offered me his hand, and while I found myself blushing at a few rude remarks from the others I didn't really mind.

'Where are we going?'

'You'll see. You're not in your kit for nothing.'

He had a firm grip on my hand, which felt tiny in his, making it all the easier to give in as I was led through a rear entrance to the bar and in under the stadium itself. My stomach felt tight and my heart had begun to pound, but I told myself I was being paid and had no choice but to do as I was told. As he pushed open a door the smell of hot male sweat made me gasp and I saw that I was in a changing room, still damp with steam from being used after that afternoon's game, with the floor glistening wet in places and discarded clothing lying on the benches of well-scrubbed wood.

I found my sense of weakness growing, as well as my reaction to the overwhelming sense of masculinity. My nipples had popped out to make two stiff little bumps under my football shirt, while I already felt hot and wet between my thighs. When Kojo eased me down onto my knees in front of one of the benches I gave no resistance at all, nor when he unzipped his fly to pull out a thick dark cock, which he fed straight into my mouth. I could barely accommodate him, but I did my best, peeling his foreskin back to suck on the big fleshy head within as I masturbated him into my mouth. He seemed to like the treatment, sitting back with a long sigh before taking me by the hair to make sure there was no escape as I did my best to please him.

He was hard in no time, his cock a great thick pole of male meat, making me ever more eager to suck, and for what I knew would come later. I pulled up my top to show him my breasts and signal that I was completely willing, at which he reached out to stroke my flesh and pull on my nipples as I worked on his erection. All my doubts and misgivings had gone, my body responding just as well as it ever had with an ordinary partner, but with the added thrill of knowing I was expected to give of my best and to make myself available in whatever way I was told.

When Kojo lifted me up under my arms and told me to turn around I simply obeyed, and even as he ordered me to pull down my shorts in front of him there was no real hesitation. I'd always found it hard, before, to show myself off the way men like, but not this time. I stuck out my bottom, looking back with what I hoped was a cheeky smile, as I pushed my thumbs into the waistband of my football shorts. He was grinning, his eyes fixed to my rear view, one hand on his beautiful cock, stroking himself, as I eased down my shorts.

I had no panties on, leaving my bottom bare in front

of him, thrust out just inches from his towering erection, with my wet cunt plainly visible between my thighs. That was all the encouragement he needed, and more. His huge, powerful hands closed on my hips and I was lifted, as easily as if I'd been a baby, onto his lap and onto his cock. I felt the big solid head I'd been sucking on press to the mouth of my sex, opening me, and slide slowly inside, big enough to make me gasp as I filled up.

He told me to spread my legs as he eased me down onto his cock and once again I obeyed immediately, pushing down my shorts and opening my thighs across his so that I was sitting in his lap. His hands moved higher to cup my breasts, stroking and pinching at my nipples as I wriggled my bare bottom into his crotch. He was right in, his balls pressed to my pussy in the most delightful way, so that with my bum stuck well out I could rub myself on him as we fucked. At that he slapped my bottom, his polite reserve giving way for the first time as he called me a dirty little bitch.

I was fine with that, and anything else he wanted to call me, just as long as I had his magnificent cock in my body, and, as my fucking went on, I was begging him to make it harder and faster. He obliged, bouncing me on his cock until I was gasping and squirming my cunt onto his balls, right at the edge of orgasm, only for him to suddenly pick me up, still stuck on his cock, and march across the room and dump me down over a massage table. I was panting and gasping again in seconds, more eager than ever, as he took me firmly by the hips and began to thrust into me, all the while smacking at my upturned bottom.

My shorts were around my ankles, my top up under my armpits, leaving me stark naked from my boobs all the way down to where my high yellow and black socks covered my calves. I knew how I'd look, and what I was – a dirty little tart in her dishevelled football kit being fucked from behind and enjoying every second of it. My only worry was that he'd spunk in me before I got to come myself. Not that I had any say in the matter. I was his to do with as he pleased, to treat in any way he wanted, no more than a little fuck dolly for his enormous cock.

And for his friends. I never even realised that the door had come open, until I heard male laughter behind me, then a voice complimenting Kojo on the way he was handling me. I tried to squirm around, shocked, but he still had his hands firmly locked into the flesh of my hips and I found myself helpless to resist. Another man spoke, and a third, all friends who'd been with us in the bar. I wanted to speak, to at least ask him to take it a little more slowly, but Kojo had begun to show off to his mates, deliberately thrusting himself in up my cunt so hard and so fast that I was immediately reduced to a panting, gasping mess.

They laughed to see the state I was in. Hands reached out to touch my body, caressing my breasts and stroking the cheeks of my bottom. Somebody took me by the hair, a blond young man whose name I couldn't even remember. He pulled down the zip to his fly and flopped out a big pink cock. I was told to open wide and I obeyed, unable to stop myself. He fed me his cock and I immediately started to suck. They'd spit-roasted me, a cock in my cunt and a cock in my mouth, something I'd read about, always with a mixture of envy and contempt for the girls who got it, dirty little bitches who'd give in to two men at the same time.

Now I was getting it, with one man's cock growing rapidly to erection in my mouth as another pumped into me from behind, and it looked as if I'd be getting a lot more than two. Both the other men had their cocks out of their trousers and were stroking themselves as they watched me get my fucking and all too obviously waiting their turn. I was going to get it, whether I liked it or not, cock after cock thrust into my body, in one hole or another, until I'd satisfied all four of them, maybe more. It was going to be more as well, several more, with new men crowding into the changing room, laughing and joking, to watch Kojo's tart getting her fucking and every single one eager for his own go.

When Kojo came he did it all over my bottom, pulling out at the last possible moment to grab his cock and deliberately making an exhibition of himself as spurt after spurt of hot thick come splashed out over my bare cheeks. His friends cheered and clapped, some openly admiring, others making noises of mock disgust, but all plainly delighted at his show of virility and the way he'd soiled me. Not that they were giving him precedence, or in the least put off by the mess. The moment he'd stepped back three of them were jostling for the right to fuck me, their erections ready for my cunt.

I wasn't even asked. One of them, the team captain who I knew only as Brazil, simply staked his claim, telling his friends to wait their turn as he pushed them aside, then sinking his cock balls-deep in my ready cunt. I still had my mouth full of cock, and was struggling to masturbate two others who pushed close in and placed my hands on their erections. It was just as well I was willing. They didn't care, using my body between them as they called out in dirty delight for the way I looked, stripped from chest to calves and jerking to the thrusts of the men inside me as their teammates' spunk trickled slowly down my bottom.

A moment later, the man in my mouth came too, jamming his cock deep and tightening his grip in my hair to the point of pain as he spunked up in my throat. I swallowed as best I could, grimacing at the bitter salty taste but happy to have been given what he had for me. However, almost before I could gulp in a breath of man-scented air I had another cock stuck in my mouth, all the way to my tonsils. My throat rebelled, squeezing on the fat helmet wedged into my gullet as I started to gag, but he merely grunted and shoved himself deeper still, leaving me in pop-eyed, breathless anguish for a matter of seconds before I was given a second full load of spunk down my throat.

I was left gasping and spitting, with spunk hanging from my nose and dribbling down my chin, fighting for breath even as I struggled to cope with the captain's hard thrusts into my cunt. They didn't care. Yet another man who I didn't even know quickly refilled my mouth and I was back on the spit-roast once more. One of the men in my hand lost control, sending a great jet of spunk high in the air to splash down across my top and in my hair, then a second, all over my back and bottom. The man in my mouth pulled out to deliberately do it over my head and left me with my face streaked with spunk and no longer daring to open my eyes. They cheered him for his filthy behaviour and then yet another cock was thrust into my open mouth, just as some blessed man ducked down to get his mouth to my cunt.

He licked me as the captain pumped his cock into my hole, and must have been in serious danger of getting an unexpected mouthful of prick from his teammate, but I no longer cared what they did, to me or to each other, as long as I continued to get a good, hard fucking while

I was licked. I felt the captain slip free and I knew he'd come inside me, but that didn't stop his friend, now lapping hard at my clit, as I sucked urgently at the cock in my mouth. I felt myself start to come, my whole body going tight as the first spasm hit me, and a second, to leave me thrashing on their cocks as I was brought off.

I'd come, leaving me weak and dizzy with reaction, but it made no difference to them. They continued to use me, now no more than their fuck toy, my body limp as they thrust into me, using my cunt and mouth, and when I'd been turned on my back, my boobs and even my armpits. I didn't know how many of them there were, only that I was going to have to satisfy every single one of them before they were done with me. My body ached, my skin was slippery with spunk, my hair ruined, my little yellow and black football kit torn and soiled, but still they used me, cock after cock inserted into every orifice they could get at, until finally they stood away to let one last man get at me, the team manager, who took advantage of my slippery bottom crease to poke the head of his cock into my anus and bring himself off up my bum.

He was the last, leaving me spreadeagled in a pool of come and sweat, barely able to move for what had been done to me, and yet I found my hands creeping back between my thighs. I began to masturbate, utterly shameless in front of the men who had used me so badly, rubbing my eager little cunt with my thighs wide open and my spare hand clutching at my slippery spunk-soiled tits. They seemed surprised at first, laughing and calling me a slut for my behaviour, but then they began to clap to a slowly rising rhythm, which reached its peak to the sounds of my screams as I came for a second time.

I was done, exhausted, sore, dizzy with sex, so far gone I couldn't even be bothered to get up. They helped, carrying me across to the big communal bath and washing me clean, helping me dry and get into my original clothes, before treating me to more champagne and finally giving me the money I'd earned. I was limping a bit when I finally left the club, my sole thought the welcome embrace of cool clean sheets in my bed, only to find my way blocked by a short, fat individual with a completely bald head and glasses. He was holding a bunch of daffodils and his face was set in an expression of hopeful lechery.

'Excuse me, but are you Sarah? Tina said I might find you here. She's busy this evening, you see, and couldn't make it. I'm Mr Ridley.'

Appleton Avenue
Elizabeth Coldwell

Don dropped her off at the house on Appleton Avenue just before nine. She gave him a kiss before he drove away, as casual as if she were going to spend an hour with her best friend, rather than a man she'd never met before. A man willing to pay for the privilege of fucking her.

Looking at the bland, brick frontage of number 22, Sharon saw nothing to set it apart from the other homes on the street. Same plain white uPVC windows and doors, same satellite dish pointing to the sky, same neat square of front garden. Nothing to indicate the man who lived here spent his time looking for sex partners on websites like the one where he'd spotted Sharon's picture and listing.

How many times had he reread that listing before sending the email requesting her services? Or was he the impulsive type, taking one look at her cloud of peroxide curls and her big tits that all but spilled from her cheap red lacy bra and deciding on the spot she was the one he wanted?

She pressed the doorbell, hearing its two-note chime echo on the other side of the door. The pause between her ring and his answer gave her a moment to wonder again quite how she'd found herself turning tricks on an amateur basis. It wasn't as though she and Don needed the money; his job on the railways was well paid, as secure as anything could be in these uncertain times. No, she did it because she enjoyed it, pure and simple: loved the thrill of stripping in front of strangers, of letting them use her pussy, her mouth, even her arse if they were willing to pay the extra. And Don loved it, too.

Sharon thought of him, no doubt already sitting in the pub round the corner, pint of mild on the table before him, nursing the hard-on he'd had since she'd slipped into her outfit for tonight. As ever, he'd tried to persuade her to give him a wank before they left, but she liked to leave him stewing in his delirious frustration. She felt reassured just thinking of his presence, close enough to call if things turned nasty. Not that they ever had, but you simply never knew.

What would she do without her darling Don? He was her safety net, her rock, her willing cuckold ...

The sound of the door swinging open distracted her

from her thoughts. 'Joe?' she asked the man who stood in the threshold. He had the advantage, of course; he'd seen almost everything she had to offer in her website photos. She gained a brief impression of serious height and a wide-shouldered torso, black hair shaved down almost to the scalp, mimicked by the stubble coating the man's chin, as he ushered her inside.

'Sharon. Great to see you. On time, too.' The way he spoke made it seem as though he'd had previous experiences of bad timekeeping, maybe even women who didn't bother to show up. That wasn't Sharon's style. Thoughts of this evening's appointment had been making her pussy prickle with lust all day, and she'd had no intention of baling out before she'd sampled everything this big rough-looking stranger had to offer.

'Nice house you have,' she murmured politely, following him through to the kitchen.

'Can I get you a drink?' Joe asked. 'Or would you like to ... er ... get straight down to it?'

He's nervous, she thought. He might look like he could snap you in half, but underneath it all, he's trembling. 'If you've got a gin and tonic, that would be lovely.'

Sharon shrugged her coat off her shoulders while Joe bustled about, pouring gin into a heavy-bottomed glass before adding a splash of tonic. When he turned round, his eyes almost bugged out of his head. She'd dressed exactly to his specifications, but still he presented the disbelieving look of a man who saw his fantasies made flesh for the first time.

As requested, she hadn't worn a bra beneath the white shirt she'd knotted just under her breasts, and her nipples were all too prominent through the thin cotton, hard brown nubs that couldn't fail to draw the eye. The shirt had been teamed with a black pleated miniskirt and knee-high socks. On a woman of Sharon's age, closer to fifty than she cared to acknowledge, the effect should have been ridiculous; half the twenty-somethings she saw heading into town for School Disco club nights couldn't carry off the look, so why did she believe she could? But this outfit had been designed purely for private viewing by her client, and Joe's expression, now one of almost drooling lust, told her it worked on that level. More than worked, if the obvious bulge in his grey marl jogging bottoms was any indication.

'Why don't we drink these upstairs?' Sharon suggested after he'd half-filled his own tumbler with gin, aware she was on the clock. Nodding dumbly, Joe ushered her out into the hall. She expected him to lead the way, but as she climbed the stairs ahead of him, she realised he was taking the opportunity to gaze up her insubstantial skirt, to where her pink thong left her arse cheeks bare, and made only a half-hearted attempt to cover up her freshly shaved pussy lips.

On the landing, Joe took charge, pointing out his

bedroom. Must live alone, Sharon thought, noting the lack of feminine touches in the room and the complete absence of female underwear scattered around. She'd never met a woman who didn't at least occasionally step out of her panties and leave them discarded on the floor when she was dog-tired, but all she could see was a tatty porn mag poking out from under the bed, enough of the title visible to let her know it featured mature, busty women – women not unlike herself.

They'd discussed the scene in detail in their email exchanges. Joe wanted to be handcuffed to the bed, gagged with Sharon's underwear, then have his arsehole reamed with a dildo. There was a time, Sharon reflected with a wry shake of her head, when she'd have considered that unusual behaviour, to say the least. The best part of a year as a housewife hooker had changed her perceptions.

She sat on the edge of the bed, sipping her gin and tonic, the drink slightly warmer than she'd have liked but still potent enough to take the edge off any anxiety she might have been feeling.

Joe stripped with quick, efficient movements, bundling up his T-shirt and jogging bottoms before throwing them aside. Commando beneath them, his hefty cock hauled itself upright as Sharon watched, mentally comparing his equipment to her husband's, as she did with every new penis that came into her line of vision. He had Don beaten for length, if not thickness, though the slick, ruddy head was almost freakishly plump. You'd certainly feel that stretching you as it entered, she thought.

Naked, Joe made himself comfortable on the bed, with its garish zigzag-patterned duvet. A pair of handcuffs stood ready for Sharon on the bedside table; decorated with pink fun-fur, they were designed to dangle from the belt of a hen-night reveller, rather than be used for serious sex play, and she suspected Joe might accidentally free himself from their clasp if he wriggled too hard, but they'd worry about that if it happened. For now, she slotted the chain that linked them between the slats of the bedhead before securing them round Joe's wrists, fastening him in place.

There was something undeniably sexy about seeing such a big man immobilised, and juice trickled into the inadequate gusset of Sharon's thong as she gazed down on him. Reaching up under her skirt, she tugged down that thong and screwed it into a warm, damp ball before stuffing it between Joe's unprotesting lips. She'd been careful not to give him so much as a flash of her cunt as she removed her underwear, and he groaned behind his makeshift gag, clearly frustrated.

'Make them wait' had always been Sharon's motto. Delayed gratification was the sweetest, and the longer it took any man to finally receive his pleasure – whether that was Don sitting in the pub, eking out his pint as he waited to come and collect her, or Joe here, unable to do anything about the erection so clearly in demand of attention – the more he appreciated it when he got it.

Teasing Joe further, acting as though she wasn't aware of what she was doing, Sharon strolled around the bedroom, thumbing her nipples through her blouse, feeling twinges of need shoot down to her pussy. When she bent to rummage through her bag and find what she needed next, she made sure to do so with her back to him, so the silly little skirt would ride up, revealing her bare bum cheeks and the soft purse of her hairless sex to Joe's helpless gaze. His muffled moan told her exactly what he thought of the sight, and how much he longed to plunge his cock deep between those round, dimpled globes.

He'd left the choice of dildo up to her, and she'd brought one of her favourites, modelled to look exactly like some porn star or other's cock, ridged with prominent veins and with realistic balls at the bottom to act as a flange, preventing the whole toy from being lost in the recipient's arse. Not that anything so big could slip all the way inside without considerable effort. Joe was going to be pushed to his limits – maybe even beyond them – but that was what he'd asked her for, and she always obliged her clients' wishes.

Pouring lube over the condom, Sharon made a show of smearing it all along the dildo's considerable length while Joe looked on, wriggling in his bonds.

'Now, Joe, I'm going to push this big, hard cock all the way up your tight arse,' Sharon crooned, approaching the bed. 'I know how much you want this, just like I want to watch you squirming as you get the fucking of your life, but with that gag in your mouth, you're not going to be able to tell me if it all gets too much. So I'm going to take pity on you ...' Reaching into his mouth, she plucked out the wet thong. 'But that's all the mercy I'm going to show you tonight.'

With that, she pushed a lube-slippery finger into his arse, meeting less resistance than she might have expected. This couldn't be Joe's first time with extreme anal play, though why should that surprise her? After all, how much did she really know about the men who paid her for sex, however many online conversations they exchanged? When all was said and done, this was a business transaction. Her clients didn't want a so-called girlfriend experience, had no time for keeping up the pretence of sharing anything other than a quick hard fuck, and that suited her just fine.

A second finger followed the first, opening Joe up just a little wider as he humped his arse against the bedcovers. Just about ready, Sharon judged, breathing in the hot musky scent of her client's crotch and listening to his harsh, urgent breathing.

'Please,' he begged. 'Oh, please. I need to be fucked.'

'Well, since you ask so nicely ...' Sharon had just lined

the fat head of the dildo up against Joe's hole, preparing to press it home, when the bedroom door opened.

'What the fuck do you think you're doing?' an angry female voice shrieked.

Sharon turned her head, seeing the blurred motion of a woman clad in a dark skirt suit striding towards her. She glanced at Joe, who slumped in his restraints, mouth gaping open – in lust or shock she couldn't tell – then back at the intruder, but not quickly enough to avoid the slap that came her way, the flat of the woman's palm connecting hard with her cheek.

'Who are you and what the hell are you doing in my house?' the woman demanded.

'I–I didn't know. Joe never –' Sharon stammered.

'I'm sorry, Sharon,' Joe said. 'Debbie wasn't supposed to be back from her conference till tomorrow.' Looking across at the woman, Joe continued, 'Debbie, love, I'm sorry. If one of you will just let me out of these cuffs, I can explain.'

Debbie shook her head, not a strand of red hair escaping from the tight bun that held it in place. 'Oh no. You're not going anywhere till we've sorted all this out. First of all, you, madam. Tell me why I walk in to find you about to stick a dildo the size of a telegraph pole up my boyfriend's arse?'

In a situation like this, Sharon knew, you have the choice of fighting or fleeing, and something about this shrewish, cocksure redhead made her determined to fight her corner. 'Because he's paying me to,' she replied defiantly.

'You what?' Debbie turned to Joe in disbelief. 'You mean while I'm slaving away to try to keep our heads above water, you're wasting our hard-earned money on some tired old slut of a prostitute?'

That stung. 'Listen here, missy. I'm not tired, and I'm definitely no slut,' Sharon snapped.

'Really? So what would you call yourself, turning up dressed like this?'

'Your husband's fantasy,' Sharon retorted. Warming to her theme, she continued, 'Just look at the magazines your beloved boyfriend hides under the bed. I'm just what he wants. Big tits, a big arse and a filthy imagination –'

Debbie launched herself at Sharon, who braced herself for another slap to the face. Instead, the younger woman grappled with her, catching hold of the front of her blouse and wrenching it open. Buttons pinged across the bedroom as Debbie tore at the fabric, baring Sharon's tits completely.

'So that's what he wants, eh?' Debbie pulled the blouse off Sharon's shoulders, before aiming a slap at each of her round, heavy breasts. The marks of her fingers were clearly visible for a moment, the stinging pain giving way to a sensual pulsing deep in Sharon's cunt.

'Debbie, calm down, love,' Joe said, but his girlfriend paid no attention to his pleas.

She grabbed Sharon's skirt. Its elasticated waistband made it easy for her to rip off, pulling it down round Sharon's knees. Debbie's eyes widened at the sight of the gold rings glittering in Sharon's sex lips.

'Maybe that's where I'm going wrong,' Debbie muttered, half to herself. 'Maybe I should get my pussy pierced, eh, Joe? Would you like that?'

This had gone far enough, Sharon thought, trying to regain her composure after being stripped almost naked by Joe's irate girlfriend. She thought of her cell phone, still stuffed in the pocket of her coat, downstairs in Joe's living room. All she had to do was ring Don; he'd come straight round and get her and this whole incident could be forgotten. If only the feelings of foolishness and humiliation at finding herself standing there in nothing but knee socks weren't changing into something more thrilling, more sexual. Despite the instincts telling her to get out of there now, she needed to be fucked.

Debbie, however, seemed to have other ideas. As Sharon made to retrieve her dildo and bag, she grabbed her by the arm. 'Where do you think you're going?'

'Look, it's better all round if I just leave. Let you and your boyfriend talk this out between you.'

'Oh, you'll be leaving all right, slut, but not right this minute. I did think about throwing you out into the

135

street, naked, but then I realised it'd be more fun if you got a taste of your own medicine, and then I threw you out into the street.'

'Hey, there's no need to go that far.' Sharon looked over to Joe for support, and found none. His cock still poked up, as hard as ever. Maybe his fantasies included catfights and forced nudity, too?

Debbie's expression was set in a chilly smirk. 'There's every need. Get on the bed – now!'

With that, she gave Sharon a shove that sent her sprawling, her face landing so close to Joe's crotch she fought the urge to stick out her tongue and run it over his balls. She tried to raise herself to a sitting position, but Debbie pushed her back down. 'Stay there. That's just how I want you.'

Sharon heard the sound of a drawer being opened and rifled through, then rustling noises and what sounded like a snap fastening being slotted into place. When she finally dared look over her shoulder, an unexpectedly horny sight greeted her. Naked from the waist down, her hair freed from its bun and flowing loose to her shoulders, Debbie had strapped a dildo harness around herself. Jutting from it was Sharon's own toy, still glistening with the lube she'd applied in preparation for sticking it up Joe's arse. She looked magnificent, and Sharon felt her pussy creaming as Debbie strode towards her.

Submissively, she raised her rump, not even needing

to be told to assume the position. Without a word, Debbie shuffled into place behind her. When the dildo bumped against her arsehole, she wondered for a scary, exciting moment whether Debbie was about to fuck her in that tight, unprepared hole, but then the toy moved lower.

It slipped into her cunt with very little effort, gliding in on the combination of lube and her freely flowing love juices.

'How do you like that, slut?' Debbie asked. 'I thought you'd be tighter, but obviously all those cocks you take have had an effect.'

The crude, sneering words only inflamed Sharon's lust further and, as Debbie started to fuck her, manicured fingers holding on tightly to Sharon's hips and rocking back and forth with swift, shallow strokes, she almost sobbed with the pleasure of it all.

Joe looked up at her, pleading with his eyes for some attention, and she bobbed her head obediently to wrap her lips round his huge, salty crown. When she'd arrived at Appleton Avenue earlier, she'd never dreamed this was how her evening would end: being dominated by a woman almost half her age, a thick dildo ploughing into her cunt and her mouth full of cock. But she couldn't think of anywhere else she'd rather be, as she laved Joe's hard length with her tongue, every thrust of the dildo inside her pushing her a little further onto his shaft.

Not caring what the consequences might be, she

reached underneath herself, located her clit and rubbed it with rapid, jabbing motions. Debbie must have been getting some stimulation from the base of the dildo against her own clit, pushing her towards orgasm, because her movements were getting faster, less assured, and she was making an odd little keening noise in her throat every time she thrust. Joe groaned, announcing he was about to come in the moment before squirts of hot spunk filled Sharon's mouth. Lost in the sights and sounds of the couple reaching their peaks, Sharon could do nothing but follow them, her vision clouding briefly and her body shaken with strong, wrenching spasms as her cunt clutched at the fat plastic shaft buried within her.

Time seemed to hang in suspension for a long moment, then the three collapsed on each other, shattered by the strength of their climaxes, the fake cock slipping from Sharon's pussy as Joe's virile, slowly wilting one slipped from her mouth.

* * *

Debbie was the first to recover, unfastening the strap-on harness and rolling off the bed to fetch the handbag she'd dropped in the doorway when she'd first arrived. Reaching inside, she opened her purse and brought out a handful of notes. 'There you go, Sharon,' she said, counting out the agreed fee and adding another twenty on top. 'I'm sorry about ruining your clothes, but the extra should more than cover the cost. I just never expected to have such a strong reaction to seeing our fantasy come to life.'

Sharon mumbled something in reply, still dazed by the power of her orgasm. She picked up her dildo, shining now with her own juices, and tossed it into her handbag, leaving the room with only a backward glance to where Joe, his hands now free of the flimsy cuffs, cuddled his girlfriend and rained kisses down on her.

My first couple, Sharon thought, stumbling down the stairs. And what an adventure that was. She almost wished she'd agreed to meet Don in the pub, instead of waiting in front of the house for him. The thought of walking the short distance wearing nothing but her coat, and arriving to share all the details of how, just as arranged, Debbie had arrived home to catch her in the act, made her feel horny all over again. Maybe he'd have got so excited, he'd have dragged her into the gents' and fucked her over the cistern, not caring whether any of the pub's other customers could hear her shrieks of delight.

She was glad Debbie had decided against taking her up the arse. Don could have that pleasure as she told him every last detail of how she'd been stripped, humiliated then screwed so beautifully by the dominant young woman. Maybe he'd slip on a cock ring before he fucked her, so he could really string out his climax – and hers. And maybe when he'd come, deep in her rear passage, she'd turn on the computer, log in and see if any other hot, kinky young couples were looking to hire a willingly submissive housewife hooker.

How to Make Money as a Hooker Wife and Amateur Porn Star
Valerie Grey

My husband videotapes me being fucked by other men who pay to watch. I get fucked by three or four different men every week and at $300 a shot and it is a substantial addition to our income – and tax free.

I first got started in this business when my husband, Alex, caught me fucking his brother, Bill. Alex was supposed to be out of town on business and Bill came over to the house to borrow my husband's video camera. I showed my brother-in-law how to set the equipment up and then played back a tape that was still in the camera. To my surprise and embarrassment, the tape was one that Alex had made of me doing a striptease for him. Before I could shut the machine off, Bill got a good close-up view of me taking off my bra. I apologised to him and was shocked even more when he said he'd like to see the rest of the tape. I had always wondered what it would be like with Bill; he is bigger and better looking than his brother. Without thinking about the consequences, I asked Bill if he'd like me to perform the striptease for him.

He nodded.

Before I could remove my panties, Bill had his big cock in his hand and was jerking off while he watched. I told him that he didn't have to jack off, that he could fuck me if he wanted. Bill ended up screwing my brains out right there on the living room sofa! My brother-in-law had his huge cock buried in my pussy and was sucking on my tits when Alex walked in the door.

My husband just stared as his brother pulled his long cock from my wet pussy. Bill stood over me while I remained lying on the sofa, panting. I was just on the verge of having an amazing climax when Bill pulled out and I couldn't catch my breath.

Alex said, 'Well, *well*. My sweet wife and my *dear brother*, here, fucking like silly rabbits!' Bill was about to say something and Alex interrupted him with, 'No, no, don't try to explain. I'm not going to get mad. In fact, seeing that big pecker of yours, dear brother, fucking Jane's pussy, well, it turned me on. What can I say, eh? Now I've got just one request. You can go back to fucking my lovely wife if you let me tape it, OK? What do you say?'

Bill's mouth gaped open and he didn't say anything. I was so worked up I blurted, 'Do it! Come on, Bill! I *need* that cock of yours! *Fuck me!*'

Bill kneeled down on the sofa, between my legs, and reinserted his stiff cock into my ya-hoo. I humped my cunt up at him, forcing more of his dick into me.

My husband taped the whole incredible scene. He zoomed in on his brother's cock as it slammed in and out of my cheating cunt. He made comments like, 'Yes! That's beautiful! A perfect shot,' and 'Suck on those tits, Bill! Drive her crazy!'

I was *going* crazy and a crushing orgasm sent fire up my spine and blanked out my mind like an EMP bomb. Bill grunted and unloaded his sperm deep inside me. Alex went, 'Pull out! Pull out of her cunt and let me get a shot of you coming on her!'

Bill jerked his pulsing cock from my twat and spewed more of his sperm onto my abdomen and cunt. Alex focused in on the splooge wads that clung to my pussy hair and dribbled down my lower stomach. He was excited, going, 'Just *look* at all that come! And look! It's oozing out of her dirty fuckhole!'

Alex and I have watched that tape many times and he still gets turned on each time we see it. Bill had Alex make him a copy and he had the nerve to show it to a friend of his! That's how I met my first trick. You see, the guy that Bill showed the tape to said, 'I'd pay good money to get some of that.'

Bill told my husband about it and Alex asked me if I'd fuck a total stranger on tape. I wasn't too keen on the idea at first but after Alex told me I'd make a couple hundred dollars doing it, I was like hell, why not. My husband told Bill to set the thing up.

Bill showed up the next evening with his friend. The guy's name was Gus and he wasn't bad looking. He couldn't take his eyes off me and I could tell he was very anxious about getting started. Alex set up the camera in our bedroom while I stripped down to bra and panties. My new 'john', Gus, waited in the living room with Bill. When Alex said everything was ready, he called for Gus. I stood next to the bed and posed, seductively. He was practically tripping over his tongue and I was really getting into playing the role of a prostitute or porn actress or whatever. When I saw my husband collect the money from Bill's friend, like he was my pimp or something, I realised I wasn't playing a role any more.

I was now a true hooker ...

* * *

Alex got behind his camera as Gus strolled over to me. Bill took a chair in the corner and settled in for his own

144

private show. I asked Gus if he liked what he saw. He touched his fingers to my bra, feeling my breasts through the cotton material. I looked at his trousers and saw his hard-on pushing down his leg.

I put my hand on the man's bulge and said, 'My, my! What's *this* you've got here, Gus?' I gave him a sexy smile. 'Why don't you help me take this tight old bra off, Gusy-Gus?'

His arms encircled me and I felt his fingers fumble with the bra clasp. I was busy undoing his belt and unzipping his trousers. Just as the elastic of my bra snapped free, Gus's pants fell to the floor. I pulled the straps off my shoulders and peeled the bra cups from my boobs. Gus became extremely excited and kicked his shoes off, stepped out of his trousers, bent and took his socks off, then removed his shirt. He had only his boxer shorts left on and his stiff dick was visible through the fly opening. I was as aroused as Gus was and couldn't wait to get my hand around his cock.

Gus hefted my tits and gently rubbed his thumbs over my nipples. In a tense voice he said, 'You cannot *believe* how much I've wanted to get my hands on these tits of yours. Ever since Bill showed me that tape of you and him, I knew I just *had* to feel these magnificent boobs.'

I reached inside his shorts and grabbed his hot stiff cock and said, 'This is a nice cock you have here, Gus! Tell me: did you jerk yourself off after seeing Bill fuck me?'

Gus could hardly speak any more but he managed to say, 'I jacked off several times ...'

I stepped away from him and said, 'Why don't you take those shorts off and then take my panties down?'

The shorts were stripped off in a flash and Gus knelt in front of me and took hold of the top seam of my panties. He pulled down slowly and groaned as my pussy hair was uncovered. He continued to pull the panties down off my hips and when he saw how they clung to my wet slit he said, 'Your pussy is soaking wet ... your panties are covered with your juices ...'

Gus pulled the panties down my legs and I stepped out of them. He stood back up and I took hold of his throbbing throbber.

I said, 'Your cock is so nice. Do you want to fuck me with it?' I looked at my husband and saw he was busy zooming in on my hand as I slowly stroked Gus's cock. Bill was still sitting in the chair but his pants were down and he had his huge cock in his hand.

Gus was almost out of control. He had one hand on my tit and the other probing my cunt. I needed to have his cock and said, 'How are you going to fuck me? How do you want to take me?'

Gus let my tit fall and said, 'From behind. I want to fuck your hot cunt from behind.'

I climbed up onto my bed and got positioned for Gus's rear entry. Alex yelled out from behind the camera, 'Turn your ass a little this way. I want a close-up of that primed cunt before it gets fucked!'

I moved my ass towards the camera and looked back to my husband saying, 'How's this?'

Alex shouted, 'Great! I've got a perfect shot of your juicing twat. Now, Gus, get up on the bed and point your cock at my wife's pussy. I want to get a shot of the head of your dick at the opening to her cunt.'

Gus crawled up behind me and steadied himself by placing one hand on the small of my back. I felt him hold his cock up to the lips of my cunt. He moved the head around in small circles until it was nestled between my pussy lips.

My husband told Gus that he had a perfect view and to go ahead and fuck me. He truly was a porn director now. I felt Gus's hands on my ass cheeks and then he eased into me. I moaned with the sensation of having the cock steadily move up my cunt. He pushed lightly on my upper back, indicating that he wanted my face down on the pillow. As I lowered my upper body, I felt my ass tilt up and my cunt slip further onto the meat stuck in me. Gus began his fuck strokes slow until his balls lay against my cunt, and then even slower pull outs, until the head of his cock was just inside me.

Alex said that the action he was taping was, 'Fan*ta*stic!' He said, 'That's terrific, Gus. What a shot of all that slick cunt slime coating your cock.'

I turned my head on the pillow and saw Bill jacking himself off. He saw me watching him and said, 'What a fucking cunt you have, Jane!'

Alex said, 'I'll only charge you two hundred bucks the next time!' He laughed.

Gus got into a steady fucking motion and grunted with each inward plunge. I came with a boiling climax and screamed into the pillow, but before the sensations were over, Gus fired his sperm deep in my contracting cunt. When he pulled out of me, I heard my husband say, 'Great! Now let me zoom in on that cunt for the "after" shot. What a mess that pussy is! It looks totally fucked.'

Bill was still jacking off in his chair, then he groaned and shot his come wad out and onto the carpet. I must admit, my first professional fuck left me totally satisfied.

* * *

I do all sorts of things these days. I mean I don't just fuck other men for money. I'll do almost anything they ask as long as it's reasonable and the price is right. There is this one older gentleman: he's 72, likes to jerk off while I show him tapes of me getting buggered by some big stud. He pays me $50 just to show him my tapes and tell him things like 'How I love big cocks coming in my cunt,' or 'How much sperm the Jamaican man shoots into me.' I've come to like the old guy and sometimes I'll even give him a hand job while he plays with my tits. He always ends up sperming all over my face, neck and tits. There's this other guy who pays $150 for me to suck his cock until he's almost ready to come and then jacks off over my ass and covers it with his thick goo. Another man pays $100 to stick his tongue in my ass while I jack him off. Everyone has their kinks.

I've become quite the experienced whore and know a lot about pleasing a man.

And there are the young men, eighteen to twenty. One, I felt kind of sorry for him. He had saved for a whole summer to get his first lay from me and all he had was $115. I told him that since he had worked so hard for it I'd give him a very special time to remember. My husband wasn't home, so I gave the kid a few tapes of me to watch while I prepared myself for him. I went to the bedroom and took all my clothes off. I put on some very tiny panties and then a very sheer negligee that allowed my tits to be seen beneath. When I went back to the living room, Nathan was watching me on the television screen. It was a scene of me screaming while a big black man fucked me senseless. I surprised him, saying, 'Oh! I'll never forget that one. He was so rough. I really thought he might tear me apart the way he was going at me.'

149

He turned to see me standing there and his eyes popped when he saw how I was dressed. He jumped to his feet and then became quite embarrassed when he saw me stare at the bulge in his jeans. I gave him a wink and said, 'Is that a hard-on you got for me?' I told him to come into the bedroom with me. Once there, I held the boy's hand and said, 'Now, don't be nervous. Take off your clothes and then come over to the bed with me.' Still, he was nervous, but he was out of his clothes in no time. I watched him walk towards the bed with his rock-hard cock leading the way. The boy's dick was pink and the head was almost purple! It was nice-sized too, a good eight inches long anyway. I sat on the bed, said to him, 'That's a very nice-looking cock you have there.' I opened the front of my negligee, exposing bare tits, and asked, 'Would you like to feel my boobs?' I saw his hard-on twitch as he fixed his stare on my jugs. I said, 'Go ahead, put your hands on my tits. I want you to hold them and squeeze them.' He stepped closer and touched the sides of my tits and then felt them in his palms. I asked, 'Do you like them? Do you like feeling my tits?' He nodded his head up and down and continued staring at them as he pressed his fingers into my full breasts. I was getting hot myself from looking at his stiff cock and from the attention he was giving my tits. I reached out and closed my hand around the shaft of the young cock. The boy gave out an excited yell and then his cock shot off. The first jet of hot semen hit right between my tits. The next spurt hit his left hand and my right tit. Two more streams splashed onto my stomach before the young man was finished. He bowed his head in disappointment. I said, 'Now, don't let that bother you. It's only normal for you to come like that when you get as excited as you are. I'm really flattered. To know that I can make a man come that easily is really quite a compliment.'

My attempt to relieve his despondency worked. He sat on the bed beside me and as I wiped his splooge from my tits and stomach, his cock began to stiffen again. I said, 'Getting hard again, are we? Well, this time I think we'll be able to keep that nice cock of yours hard for a long time.' I got out of bed and slowly removed my negligee.

He watched me intently and said, 'You're so beautiful ...'

I thanked the young man and then turned my back to him, asking, 'Would you mind taking my panties down for me?' He didn't say a word as I bent forwards, presenting my ass to him. I felt his hands on my waist. Then his fingers worked between the fabric of my panties and my skin. The young man's breathing was becoming heavy as he pulled the thin material down over my ass. When the panties were just below my rounded ass cheeks, the boy's breathing stopped.

151

He pulled the nylon panties down to my thighs and then said, 'Your pussy ... it's so big and hairy ... the way it sticks out behind you ...'

I told my excited young man to finish taking my panties off and he did. Keeping my back to him, I moved one foot to the side to give a better view of my cunt.

I said, 'Do you want to feel my pussy? Go ahead, put your hand on it, touch it.'

His fingers lightly brushed my cunt hair and then closed on my meaty twat.

I let out, 'Feel how hot my cunt is. Open my pussy lips and feel how hot and wet the inside is.'

His fingers worked through the pubic hair and then separated the halves of my snatch. I felt his fingers slipping into me. I turned around to face him, sitting on the edge of the bed. His young cock was standing straight up from his lap.

I leaned over to kiss him and his hands came up to catch my swaying tits. I took hold of his hard-on and felt all along the length of it. It was hot and pulsing with his pounding heart.

Nathan broke off our kiss and said, 'Can—can I fuck you now?'

I squeezed on his hard dick and said, 'Yes, you can fuck me now. I want to have your nice hard cock fucking me. Do you want to fuck me doggie style? You know, from behind?'

He nodded his head to say yes and said, 'I want to do it like I saw you on that tape. The one where that big black man fucked you while you were on your hands and knees.'

I replied, 'You get behind my ass on the bed and slide this nice big cock into my hairy cunt.' I positioned myself on the bed and waited for my young lover to get behind my ass. He softly rubbed his hands over my ass and then up my sides to my hanging tits. I felt his cock poking into the crack of my ass as he stretched over my back.

He let my tits fall free and straightened up to a kneeling position between my legs, and up against the cheeks of my ass. I reached a hand between my legs and spread open my slick pussy lips. I looked back at him and said, 'Oh, come on. Do it. Put your hard cock into me, baby. Come on, *fuck me.*'

He trembled a little and then put his dick at my hole. I released my cunt lips and felt them cover the head of the twitching cock. The boy held my hips and went, 'Your pussy is so hot!' He gently slid his meat into me, hissing the entire time his cock entered. I started rocking back and forth on his stiff dick, causing it to slide in and out of my gooey twat.

He got into the same rhythm with me and was soon plunging all the way into me and pulling all the way out. Suddenly he couldn't take any more and thrust his hips forwards, burying his dick deep into me. He yelled and I felt his come load spurt deep in me.

Just as he pulled out, Alex walked in and said, 'Going after young ones now, are we?'

My lover was so surprised that he nearly fell off the bed.

I told him it was OK and said to my husband, 'Alex, this is Nathan. He's been saving the whole summer to get enough money to pay for this. For his first time, he is some hot lover. He fucked me out of my mind.'

My husband grinned and said, 'Well Nathan, was it good? Did you like screwing Jane?'

Nathan stuttered, 'She is so beautiful!'

Alex said, 'Well, since that was your first time getting laid, how would you like to have my wife give you a blow job you'll never forget? I'll even tape it for you so you can show all your friends.'

Nathan blurted, 'But I won't have any more money after I give you the hundred and fifteen dollars I have.'

I looked at Alex, winked, and said, 'Nathan, the way you fucked me with that big cock of yours, I couldn't charge you for that and I'd love to show you how thankful I am by sucking your dick.'

My husband prepared to tape me giving the nineteen-year-old his first blow job while I cleaned Nathan and myself up from the mess we'd made fucking. When Alex said he was ready, I was playing with Nathan's cock and balls. I told him to stand beside the bed and I got down on my knees. I took his semi-hard cock in my hand and brought it to my lips. I put my mouth over the end of Nathan's dick and sucked it in over my tongue. I felt the smooth shaft swell and then stiffen out.

I had about half of his young meat in my mouth and my husband said, 'Deep throat him. Swallow his cock, Jane!' I opened my throat and pushed my head down onto the throbbing organ, forcing the cock head into my throat. The young man's smooth balls were hanging under my chin and my nose was stuck in his soft pubic hair. I had my arms around his hips, my fingers gripping his firm buns.

Slowly, I pulled my head back until the crown of Nathan's cock was at my lips. I looked up to his straining face and cupped his hot balls. He put his hand on top of my head and I started going back down on the slick meat. When the head of his dick entered my throat again, I slithered my tongue on the underside of his cock and then pulled back again. I made suctioning noises as I sucked. Nathan began to groan and push on the back of my head as I began bobbing on and off of his hard-on. He fucked my mouth for several more seconds and then stiffened his legs, preparing to fire his sperm down my throat. I wanted to see and feel his hot come load, so I jerked my mouth off his cock and jacked him off as fast as I could move my hand. Nathan yelped and shot a huge wad of boiling sperm directly into my open mouth. Another glob of baby batter splattered my left eye and cheek. I kept squeezing and pumping his jerking cock and took another heavy stream of come onto my nose. I put my mouth back onto his cock and took several more ejections of sperm without swallowing.

His balls emptied, I pulled off him and looked up.

My vision was blurred from the sticky come covering my eye. I had sperm dripping off my nose onto my tits. The salty semen was running out of my mouth and drooling down my chin like I was a teething infant.

My face was covered with semen.

I stared at him and licked his come from my lips, saying, 'I love it when a man shoots in my mouth and all over my face.'

We made a copy of the tape of me sucking Nathan's cock. Alex gave the nineteen-year-old the copy and said, 'Here ya' go, kiddo, this tape is for you. Hope you enjoyed everything with Jane. Remember this was a gift for your first time. Normally, a man would have had to pay close to three hundred dollars to get treated like you were.'

I didn't hear from Nathan again, but he must have showed his tape to his school friends. A couple of days after he was here, I had another young man who wanted to know how much it would cost for a hand job. I told him I'd jack him off for $25 and for an extra $10 he could play with my tits while I did it. I've fucked a couple of the boys with really muscular bodies and bigger than average cocks. Those young men shoot so quick, but they are hard again in seconds ...

* * *

I truly enjoy my new life as a paid hooker. I can't say I am a professional like I am no more a professional porn actress. My husband Alex has a collection of over a hundred and fifty tapes of me with other men. He has sold copies of three dozen of them online as 'amateur porn'. One of the most popular ones is me getting gang-banged by sixteen men.

That is another, different story ...

Pleasuring the Enemy
Lara Lancey

Celeste buttoned her black lace gloves as she hurried down the steps from Montmartre en route to the Pigalle area. How many feet had trotted up and down this hillside over the centuries to make the stone so worn? And how many steps were there altogether?

She always lost count because she was always late for her shift. Every evening Pierre and the other artists hanging around the main square distracted her, pestering her to sit for them so they could sketch her in a desperate attempt to attract business in these dark times. They were all sweet enough but she was lucky to have a job and she couldn't risk losing it.

Because once she'd finished flirting with the boys, run down those steps, along the streets and in to work,

Madame Baise would be standing at the kitchen door, tapping her watch. How furious would her mother be if she was sacked?

Not that her mother knew what the work exactly entailed. She would have fifty fits if she knew that the pastries and puddings her precious Celeste was preparing each night weren't for some respectable army officers' club or one of the select restaurants still operating off the Champs-Elysées despite the German occupation, but for the hungry clients of the most famous bordello in Paris.

Sure enough it was about five past ten when she ran through the iron gateway and into the little courtyard of La Maison Baise. But there was no sign of Madame. There were no lights or voices in the windows upstairs. No music or laughter coming from the sumptuous reception rooms downstairs. And no clattering of pots and pans in the kitchen.

'Not so late tonight, Celeste. Bravo. Come in. We're having a meeting.' Just as Celeste was turning to go, Madame Baise beckoned her into her private quarters.

'But where are the gentlemen?' Celeste peered round the quiet courtyard. 'You haven't been put out of business, have you?'

'Not exactly.' Madame Baise ushered Celeste into her private room. 'But things are going to change.'

Most of the other girls were already gathered. They

looked odd in their outdoor coats and hats. Celeste barely recognised them with their clothes on. She went and sat beside Aurore, the most popular of the girls. To be honest, she had a bit of a crush on her. She was so beautiful – white skin, black hair, glittering blue eyes ...

'We have had unofficial orders from the War Office.' Madame Baise called for hush. 'We have been told that we must rise up against the occupiers like some other *maisons closes*, and refuse to service them.'

There was a silence for a moment, and then Aurore spoke. 'But we just want to earn money! I don't care who we service, so long as they are male, and clean, and rich!'

The others murmured agreement. Celeste kept quiet. She was trying to work out if she should start applying for a new job. Only this evening Pierre had caught her as she passed behind Sacré-Coeur, and this time he'd offered her money to sit for him.

All she'd have to do is what Aurore and the others did all the time, except without the sex. She couldn't tell Maman, of course, but she would just lie on a couch in Pierre's chilly studio, pull her hair out of its pins, put on red lipstick, try to forget that she was naked and let him paint her. He was talented, she knew that, but he was also very young and very shy. He wouldn't do anything to shame her – would he?

She blushed at the thought of it. Would he try to touch her? Ask her to open her legs, or make a seductive expression? She looked younger than she was, but she was still a virgin ...

'We have to agree who our clients are to be.' Madame Baise cut through her thoughts. 'We can't have both French and German clients under the same roof. If any of you object to pleasuring the enemy, then you may leave now with my blessing.'

Nobody moved.

'What are they like up close?' asked Aurore, scratching her ankle, making the silk stocking wrinkle. '*Les boches*?'

'I've heard they're tall, blond, fit, scrupulously clean, rich –'

'Well hung?' giggled Véronique, Aurore's best friend. They all laughed, and started unbuttoning their coats. It seemed that the decision had been made. Underneath they wore their working gear: pure silk negligees in pastel colours, matching camisoles, white stockings. And nothing else. Even in the depths of winter, this is how they arrived ready for work.

'Only one way to find out!' spluttered Aurore, taking off her hat and plumping up her dark waved hair. She crossed her legs. They were the longest legs Celeste had ever seen. Pale thighs that led the eye straight up to the jet-black triangle covering her sex. No wonder she was the highest earner.

'And also they are charming.' Madame Baise coughed rather abruptly. Her cheeks were pink with excitement.

'Or so I've heard. So if you're up for it, girls, the way to avoid detection is not to take money off them ...'

Celeste twisted her hands. No money? How was she ever going to bring home rent for her mother?

'... but to let them pay us in food, clothes, perfume, alcohol – you name it!'

The girls relaxed. It was just as if nothing had changed, as if the gentlemen were already here, listening to music across the courtyard in the salon, studying the erotic paintings on the walls while they waited their turn.

Madame Baise came over to Celeste. 'You know, Celeste, if we go ahead with this, not only will we make it a female-only establishment, including the cooks and cleaners, but I will put you in total charge of the kitchen.'

'That's an honour, Madame, but I can't afford to work without money.' Celeste shook her head. 'And my mother would never allow me to work for *les boches* –'

'You're not a working girl like these others, *chérie*. Your conscience can be completely clear on that score. You will simply be feeding our new guests. So you will be paid as a head chef, in cash.' Madame Baise handed over a wad of francs. 'So tomorrow you will start off by buying steak, and vegetables, and bread, as well as your speciality pastries. I am sure our new clients will enjoy your famous *choux* and *millefeuilles* but they will want main courses as well. They might even want you to cook the German way.'

162

Those words should have sent shivers down Celeste's spine, but all she could think as she ran home was how happy her mother would be with the promotion, how horrified she would be if she knew who the new clients were, whether or not her daughter was pleasuring them. And how disappointed poor Pierre would be.

* * *

Within two days *les boches chéris*, as Aurore started calling them, had arrived for business, and Celeste was rushed off her feet. She had no chance to peek at the tall, blond, clean males. She was so exhausted some nights she even slept in the little room behind the pantry, directly under the boudoirs, drifting off to the sounds of jazz and chatter, underlaid by the more urgent sounds of fucking, the crying out of soldiers more than satisfied with their horizontal collaborators.

Men were still entering the cobbled courtyard, even though it was nearly dawn. She might have been afraid, but she never saw the invaders face to face and, in any case, whenever Madame Baise greeted new arrivals, it was the same laughter and music as before that flooded into the night

'Because sex is the same in any language,' Madame Baise said, patting her new silk dress.

One evening, Celeste had sent her juniors home. The

meat and vegetables were finished, and she was just sampling the last desserts before they went up to the dining room. Word was spreading about her skills *à la cuisine*, according to Aurore. Around her were plates and trays piled with croissants, brioches, tarts, stuffed vol-au-vents, pastries that flaked and dribbled chocolate and custard and creamy cheese.

She took her cap off, loosened her stiff collar and top buttons, and leaned over the kitchen table. She was so tired that if she sat down she would never stand up again.

She took a spoonful of lemon syllabub, spiked with the orange liqueur she had managed to get her hands on. It was heaven on a spoon. Her lips were slicked with mousse.

'*Excusez-moi, mademoiselle?*'

Celeste jumped, smearing syllabub across her cheek.

At the door was a dancing bottle of champagne.

'*Entrez!*' she whispered, clutching on to the table.

A German soldier put his head round the door. She stared at him, and he stared at her. He came further into the kitchen.

'*C'est tout délicieux!*' he said, clicking his ankles together. Then he went as red as beet. 'I have come to say thank you for the delicious food, and to ask if the chef will take a drink with me?'

She saw that the bottle was already open. He was a little drunk. But smart, blond and handsome, just as

Madame Baise had said. His verdigris uniform was pressed and the buttons shone in the bright lights. His pale-blue eyes gleamed as he held the bottle out to her.

She thought of Pierre and his friends, their joie de vivre snuffed out when they started muttering about the Resistance, scruffy as they slouched and smoked.

This man was the same age but completely different. Maybe he was once scruffy and angry, too, but war had shaped this man into something she'd never met before. Trained. Proud. Determined. And very scary.

'I'm working –'

'Madame Baise says it is permitted. In fact, she encouraged me to come down here to see you.' He pulled two glasses off a shelf and poured some wine into both. 'She thinks you're wasted down here.

'Well, I suppose my shift is nearly over.'

Celeste tipped the champagne gratefully into her throat while the young man briefly disappeared. Then he returned, shouldering open the door, and weighed down with platters of more bloody steak, muddy vegetables, fresh fruit, pots of cream, whole golden cheeses, slabs of chocolate – even a box of salty *fruits de mer*.

'Where did you get all this?'

'My superiors.' He shrugged. 'They know I love food and cooking. And we were told to pay you in food.'

Celeste exclaimed, 'But I haven't serviced you yet!'

The word 'yet' shivered in the air.

'You have serviced my stomach, *mademoiselle*, and you know where the stomach leads?' He came closer, wafting the scent of strawberries.

'So you liked my pavlova?' she trilled nervously. The champagne had gone straight to her head.

'It makes me think of summer, lying in a lush meadow.' He picked up a lone strawberry and dangled it on its green thread. 'You can smell the grass, can't you, as you spread out the picnic? Feel the sun on your legs, pull your dress up over your bare knees ...'

He pushed the fruit at her mouth.

'When did you last have a picnic with a lover, *mademoiselle*? In the open air, far away from your mother's prying eyes, or your friends. Lying back, your dress falling open, waiting for him to kiss you?'

He pushed the strawberry at her mouth again. Her lips opened very slowly to take it in.

'Go on, eat.' He lifted her chin. 'Careful it doesn't drip ...'

'Too late.' Juice dribbled over her bottom lip and onto his finger.

He wiped the finger across her mouth again. She could taste the mixture of clean skin and strawberry and it was all she could do not to suck his finger right into her mouth.

She had felt this same rushing sensation when Pierre tried to kiss her a week or so ago. Her heart had started pounding when she felt his breath on her face. Her body had started throbbing. She wanted it, but something stopped her. The rain? The smelly dark alley they were standing in, perhaps? Her mother's front door within sight?

But afterwards she had thought of it. His voice turning gruff. The things he'd said about wanting to touch her, take her clothes off, the way he'd taken her hand and guided it to the stiff bulge in his trousers. She'd squealed like a baby and run home, but when she'd tried to sleep, his words had tormented her until all she could do was run her hands over her thighs, into the warm space between them, fingers drawn over the soft lips, agitating the little hairs, slipping into the wet crack hiding there, tickling herself open, poking inside, trying to locate the throbbing that wouldn't go away, pushed further, her body tightening around her finger, felt that rising tide of desire, sensing that if she could reach the peak the throbbing would stop, pushing faster, stroking her nipples with the other hand, that heat, rising, burning, her hips bucking off the old bedstead in the attic, the views over Paris, as her fingers fucked her and then, at last, there was a kind of flashing inside her and at long last the throbbing died away …

'I don't have a lover, *monsieur*. Not a real one.' She choked slightly. 'I'm only a cook.'

'If that's true –' he trailed a finger down her hot cheek

and licked syllabub off his finger '– then you're ready for plucking.'

'Oh, there's a boy in my neighbourhood who wants me, but –' that throbbing started up again, deep behind her navel '– I've never let him kiss me. I'm not a *fille de joie* like the girls upstairs.'

'Being kissed doesn't make you a tart!' He jerked his head towards the courtyard. 'But they are damn good. So beautiful, sexy, adventurous. And older. You can even have two at the same time if you're prepared to bring enough chocolate!' He grinned. 'I had no experience before I came here.'

Celeste turned away. She was feeling faint. The kitchen was too warm. The soldier was too close. Any minute now Madame Baise would be ringing the bell for the desserts or even barging into the kitchen.

'I'm embarrassing you. Sorry.' He rubbed his hair. 'It was cooking I came to talk about, not sex.'

'So, perhaps you could tell me what to do with all this?' she stammered, pointing at the scallops. 'I'm only a pastry chef.'

He picked up a knife and expertly levered open one shell to show its pearly interior. 'Hmm. *Coquilles Saint Jacques*, I think. My pièce de résistance. Let me make a cheese sauce, and then I'm going to feed you, because you look too thin and pale. Scallops first, then steak.'

The dining-room bell rang and Celeste bustled to the

servery with the final tray of desserts. When she came back he had his jacket off and was hunched over the wooden board, whisking cream, grating cheese, taming misshapen vegetables. She watched the muscles flexing in his strong arms and out of the blue came the thought of him smothering her in warm butter. Flipping her over like a pancake.

'I'll just freshen up,' she murmured, backing towards the pantry.

He slapped the steaks down onto the griddle. They sizzled urgently, smoke and steam rising into his face, making his hair fall into his eyes and turning Celeste's kitchen into a heavenly hell.

She stared into the old tarnished mirror. A pale face, no rouge, hair scraped back after an evening's cooking. Black eyes and curvy body, but otherwise a complete contrast with Aurore and the others who were like glorious painted exotic birds. She pinched her cheeks to get some colour, bit her lips to make them red. Took off her apron. That throbbing in her belly was edging downwards ...

Back in the kitchen the champagne was in a bucket. There were two plates, each with a steak lying inside a star shape of leeks and drenched in a pale-green sauce. A square stack of cut potatoes was beside these, glittering with salt.

He wasn't there. The disappointment was like a slap,

but she was starving. Celeste sat down and couldn't help herself. She leaned over the table and stuffed some fried wedges into her mouth. The golden potato skins burst against her teeth to release the buttery, fluffy centres. She cut into the steak, letting the sauce linger on her tongue.

Behind her, a low laugh. The German had come back into the room with some wine. His shirt was still pristine, but the steam had bounced his hair into boyish curls and he'd let down his braces.

'*Délicieux, monsieur,*' Celeste enthused with her mouth full. She felt safest talking about food.

'Call me Johan.'

The foreign name was like a slap of danger, but it was a pleasant slap. Exciting, even. A kind of madness came over her with each delicious bite. Celeste kept her eyes on him while she finished every morsel of steak. Then, seeing that he was not eating, she reached across and snatched his plate, making him laugh as she polished off his steak, too.

'They say you can tell what a girl is like in bed from the way she eats.'

Celeste giggled, her voice bubbly with champagne. 'So, what's for dessert?'

'Well, there's a big cream cake right here, but I think I'll have the chef.'

Johan stood up, kicking the chair back, came towards her and lifted her out of her chair. Her throat swelled in a groan but any sound was drowned by his mouth on hers, his tongue pushing her lips open, the length of his body overpowering her as he twisted her and pushed her back against the table. His hands were warm and heavy as they travelled over her and, still kissing her, making her insides molten, he pulled her blouse wide open and took hold of her breasts. Her breath caught as his fingers closed over the flimsy silk petticoat covering them. His big steak-bashing hands came up and ripped aside her bra and petticoat, pushing her breasts together, rubbing her nipples till they were sore. She yearned against him, her whole body aching and hot now, full of food, dizzy with champagne.

'I should be clearing up,' she gasped.

'They're far too busy to fuss about that.' His voice had grown deeper, just as Pierre's did that time. He pressed up against her and she leaned back against the table, yielding to the pleasure radiating from her swollen breasts. She could feel the big shape bulging in his tailored trousers pushing against her. She reached down and felt it jump under her hand. She couldn't let go. She started rubbing it, delighting in the groans deep in his throat.

Johan reached up under her skirt, his fingers strong and warm. He ripped at her French knickers. Being silk they slipped down easily. She kicked them away from tangling round her ankles and opened her legs wider so that his fingers could plunge into the soft fur of her pussy.

As he stroked and fondled her, her legs quivered. She stopped kissing him and her head fell back as those fingers teased sensation out of that virgin spot. Then he whipped her round and pushed her face down on the table, her breasts squashing straight into the big cream cake he'd left there. The aroma of vanilla and cream, and coffee curls, spread into her nostrils as she fell forwards and let him lift her skirt up right over her hips.

She heard him fumble for his trouser buttons, felt the warm sausage shape of his penis thump onto her bottom. The table jabbed into her stomach, making her light-headed as she struggled to breathe. The German muttered something under his breath, his big hands swiping over her haunches as if she were a side of prime beef. Thrills streaked through her body, to her secret place, her throbbing, empty, waiting cunt.

His hands slid up and down her hips, her skin alive under his touch. He bent her further, so that her bottom lifted in the air. She was on fire. This was how she'd reacted to Pierre's sexy words, the promise of his touch, the fiery responses that she had tamed in the privacy of her bedroom. This is how it would feel, if or when she let him do it.

Johan kicked her legs further apart and, with a chuckle, he took a handful of gateau, squeezing it in his hand, and then there was cool, wet stickiness as he smeared the cream and smashed cake up her thighs, into the crack

172

of her pussy, the scent mingling with her own scent of excitement.

'Now, let me taste you.'

She could barely hear him, he was so quiet, but he got on his knees behind her, holding her cheeks open, and she screeched as his tongue, swiping warm and wet, licked at the cream covering her pussy, tantalising the aching red bud which had popped out of its hibernation.

She flung her arms out so hard that the cake plate fell and smashed on the floor, but she just laughed out loud, *tant pis*, and then was stunned when he darted his tongue into her. The tide of pleasure grew and threatened to overwhelm her.

A woman's voice groaned into the gasping silence. 'Just fuck me!'

Little virginal Celese, so wanton now, and brazen. He laughed softly again, stood up, and there it was. His penis. *La bite*. Pierre had whispered that slang word, putting her hand on the bulge in his trousers. Johan's cock, solid and hot, was edging up the crack, then the round knob was finding its way in.

'*Vas-y*,' she groaned. 'Go on, go on!'

It's easy, so easy, all so natural. She tilted her hips for him and he slid inside. She was spread across the table like a feast, her legs sheathed in stockings but nothing else, his hands grasping her hips and pulling her against him. She could feel her cunt squeezing and twitching, wanting to swallow him whole, but as with good cooking the skill was in the waiting.

He moved slowly, pushing that rigid length luxuriously inside her. She gripped the table for balance, her breasts soaked in cake and cream, desperate now for him to ram it up her, she was so ready, so loving it, and she heard herself moaning, pleading for it. He pulled her against his body and then he was groaning, too, and they were moving as one and his warm torso was against her spine, and now she was tossing her head, slithering back and forth in the sticky mess of cake, keeping him stiff inside her, her German lover fucking her there on the kitchen table where earlier she had been cutting shapes and sprinkling sugar.

Then they were moving faster as the ecstasy reached its peak, the orgasm hovering, the kitchen table skittering across the floor, pleasure simmering and rolling, and now coming to the boil, his cock shooting into her and then her own climax exploding amongst the pots and pans of her kitchen.

There was a round of applause and laughter from the courtyard door. Framed there were Madame Baise, Aurore, Veronique and several grinning German officers.

'I knew you were wasted down here, Celeste.'

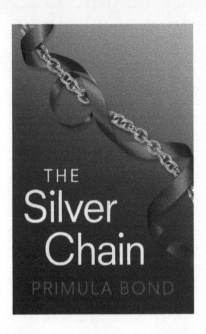

THE SILVER CHAIN – PRIMULA BOND

Good things come to those who wait…

After a chance meeting one evening, mysterious entrepreneur Gustav Levi and photographer Serena Folkes agree to a very special contract.

Gustav will launch Serena's photographic career at his gallery, but only if Serena agrees to become his companion.

To mark their agreement, Gustav gives Serena a bracelet and silver chain which binds them physically and symbolically. A sign that Serena is under Gustav's power.

As their passionate relationship intensifies, the silver chain pulls them closer together. But will Gustav's past tear them apart?

A passionate, unforgettable erotic romance for fans of *50 Shades of Grey* and Sylvia Day's *Crossfire Trilogy*.

POWER PLAY – CHARLOTTE STEIN

Now she's the boss, everything that once seemed forbidden is possible…

Meet Eleanor Harding, a woman who loves to be in control and who puts Anastasia Steele in the shade.

When Eleanor is promoted, she loses two very important things: the heated relationship she had with her boss, and control over her own desires.

She finds herself suddenly craving something very different – and office junior, Ben, seems like just the sort of man to fulfil her needs. He's willing to show her all of the things she's been missing – namely, what it's like to be the one in charge.

Now all Eleanor has to do is decide…is Ben calling the kinky shots, or is she?

Find out more at www.mischiefbooks.com

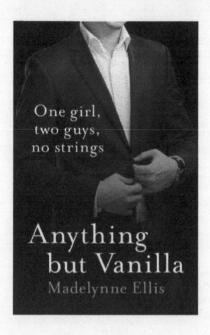

ANYTHING BUT VANILLA
MADELYNNE ELLIS

One girl, two guys, no strings.

Kara North is on the run. Fleeing from her controlling fiancé and a wedding she never wanted, she accepts the chance offer of refuge on Liddell Island, where she soon catches the eye of the island's owner, erotic photographer Ric Liddell.

But pleasure comes in more than one flavour when Zachary Blackwater, the charming ice-cream vendor also takes an interest, and wants more than just a tumble in the surf.

When Kara learns that the two men have been unlikely lovers for years, she becomes obsessed with the idea of a threesome.

Soon Kara is wondering how she ever considered committing herself to just one man.

Find out more at www.mischiefbooks.com

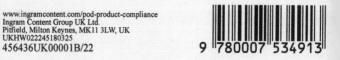